Praise for

Memories of a Marriage

"A consummately constructed monument to human imper-
fection."   —*San Francisco Chronicle*

"Engrossing . . . Begley gives us a chance to see into two different, often obscured worlds. One is the most private recesses
of another couple's marriage. The other is high-WASP
society—though most people don't usually even know where
that particular unmarked door is, let alone get a chance to
have it quietly shut in their faces. . . . The pleasures of this
novel reside not so much in where the 'truth' lies as in its
context. The world of the highly entitled at play and at
work—seen traveling the globe over the decades, installing
themselves in European hotels and joining exclusive men's
clubs and marrying into families made up of 'very much our
kind of people'—remains irresistible."
                              —*The New York Times Book Review*

"This delicious, dazzling novel about the rise and fall of a
great American debutante kept me up all night. Begley knows
everything about the secret lives of the American aristocracy,
and he tells all."   —SUSAN CHEEVER

"Absorbing ... Begley proves he is a master dissector of the American character.... He tells this tale with all the archness—and yearning—of a voyeur looking in.... His evocations of glistening mahogany in New York's club rooms, of summering in the Hamptons, of oysters and whiting at the Paris Savoy have the clear ring of truth. He has observed the relevant mannerisms, and he garnishes his scenes with all the glee of a name-dropping arriviste.... Read it and weep."

—*The Washington Post*

"Begley, an elegant stylist with a dry wit and a merciless eye ... is eloquent on the subject of Lucy."   —*The Wall Street Journal*

"Elegant and cool ... beautifully crafted ... Thanks to Mr. Begley's talented pen, we, like Philip, cannot resist becoming ... fascinated by the details of this marriage."

—*The Washington Times*

"In this compact, voyeuristic novel, Begley creates his latest larger-than-life character in the beguiling but sharp-tongued socialite Lucy De Bourgh.... Begley's effortless storytelling will have readers ... fascinated by Lucy and Phillips's complex, tangled relationship."

—*Publishers Weekly* (starred review)

"A fiendishly clever, Fitzgeraldesque tale about marriage, friendship, gossip, and self-justification ... Begley, marvelously droll and possessed of a rapier wit, revels in his mercurial characters, intricate psychological puzzles, unreliable memories, counterintuitive class divisions, and all the mysteries and miseries of lust and love." —*Booklist*

"Sharply observed and subtly nuanced ... It could pass as a novel from F. Scott Fitzgerald's later decades, if Fitzgerald had lived so long." —*Kirkus Reviews*

MEMORIES OF A MARRIAGE

BY LOUIS BEGLEY

FICTION

Memories of a Marriage

Schmidt Steps Back

Matters of Honor

Shipwreck

Schmidt Delivered

Mistler's Exit

About Schmidt

As Max Saw It

The Man Who Was Late

Wartime Lies

NONFICTION

Why the Dreyfus Affair Matters

Franz Kafka: The Tremendous World I Have Inside My Head

Memories of a Marriage

A Novel

LOUIS BEGLEY

BALLANTINE BOOKS TRADE PAPERBACKS

NEW YORK

2014 Ballantine Books Trade Paperback Edition

Copyright © 2013 by Louis Begley 2007 Revocable Trust
Reading group guide copyright © 2014 by Random House LLC

Published in the United States by Ballantine Books, an imprint of Random House, a division of Random House LLC, a Penguin Random House Company, New York.

BALLANTINE and the HOUSE colophon are registered trademarks of Random House LLC.
RANDOM HOUSE READER'S CIRCLE & Design is a registered trademark of Random House LLC.

Originally published in hardcover in the United States by Nan A. Talese / Doubleday, a division of Random House LLC, and in Canada by Random House of Canada, Limited, Toronto, in 2013.

Library of Congress Cataloging-in-Publication Data
Begley, Louis.
Memories of a Marriage : a novel / Louis Begley.
pages cm
ISBN 978-0-8041-7902-7
eBook ISBN 978-0-385-53748-3
1. Autobiographical memory—Fiction. 2. Nineteen fifties—Fiction.
3. Marriage—Fiction. 4. Psychological fiction. I. Title.
PS3552.E373M46 2013
813'.54—dc23   2012043331

www.randomhousereaderscircle.com

147028622

For Anka

All you need is love, love, love is all you need . . .

—THE BEATLES

MEMORIES OF A MARRIAGE

I

ONE EVENING IN May 2003, not many days after George W. Bush's astonishing announcement that the "mission" had been accomplished, I went to the New York State Theater to see a performance by the New York City Ballet company. I had hoped to find an all Jerry Robbins program, and there was, in fact, such a program scheduled for later that month. Unfortunately, the date was inconvenient—I had accepted a dinner invitation from a newly remarried classmate—and I had to settle for a performance that included the official premiere of *Guide to Strange Places,* one more of Peter Martins's empty creations. The music by John Adams left me indifferent. If only, I said to myself, Martins had allowed us to go on thinking of him as the magnificent dancer he had been in his prime and being grateful for his management of the company, instead of giving us again and again occasions to deplore his choreography. Unable to concentrate on the movements, brilliantly executed by the cast, that seemed to me to lead to nowhere, I allowed my thoughts to turn to Jerome Robbins. He had been my wife Bella's and my dear friend, regularly inviting us to rehearsals. We would watch him go over each segment of a ballet tirelessly: scolding, correcting, and cajoling, until a mysterious change, often imperceptible to Bella and me, signaled that the music and the dance had come together and now corresponded to his vision. He would clap his hands, turn to his assistant Victor, and say, That's it, the kids have got it, let's go and eat. Jerry was ravenously hungry after rehearsals. We would tag along with him and Victor to Shun Lee, a Chinese restaurant on West Sixty-Fifth Street, where Jerry, so abstemious in daily life, devoured one after another the mild Cantonese dishes that were his favorites. He died in 1998, fifteen years after George Balanchine, and the curtain went down on a great era in ballet history that their work had defined. I was grateful to have seen so much of it while they were still alive, danced by dancers they had formed. Would the company for which they had created so many master-pieces continue to perform them in high style? I hoped it would, at least for the remainder of my years.

At the intermission, I got a whiskey at the bar and, the weather being mild, went out on the open terrace. The fountain in the center of the plaza had not yet been redesigned and programmed to keep time to a beat as intricate as Fred Astaire's steps and no easier to decipher, but I liked it anyway and never tired of looking at it. I was bewitched. How wonderful, I said to myself over and over, how glad—really how happy—I am to have come back to live in this city! For much of my life I had dreaded admitting to myself or others that I was happy. To do so, I was certain, was to invite the gods to strike where I was most vulnerable. Not my own person, but Bella or our little Agnes. Alas, the full measure of punishment had already been meted out, leaving me diminished but invulnerable. We had been living between Paris and New York, with longer stays abroad because of Bella's family, all of whom were there. Soon after the beginning of one of our New York sojourns Agnes was killed—instantaneously—by the falling limb of a tree in Central Park, which also gravely injured the nurse who was taking her home from the Children's Zoo. Our grief was extreme. Unable to speak about the disaster for two years or more, we suffered in silence and, without need for discussion, concluded that we would not have another child; Agnes's place could not be taken, and we did not wish to give another hostage to fortune. We stayed away from New York as much as possible, learning to live for each other and for our work. We were hardly ever apart. I am a writer and so was Bella; we designated as our offices two adjoining rooms of every habitation we occupied, whether in New York City or the house on a rocky hillside outside Sharon, Connecticut, I inherited in the fifties from a maiden aunt or the apartment in Paris near the Panthéon.

Then one winter, which for professional reasons we were spending in New York, Bella, who had never complained of an ache or a pain, who never caught colds or allowed jetlag to upset her sleep pattern, whose digestion triumphed over every cuisine, began to suffer from lingering sniffles and strange little infections; red blotches appeared on her skin.

She joked that if either of us were a drug addict sharing needles or sleeping with fellow addicts she would think she had AIDS. But in her case, she said, she had simply been beaten down by the interminable New York winter. I thought she was right. For the first time in our lives we went south in search of the sun, to Barbados, the only appealing island where a place to stay that met our requirements—those indispensable two offices and close proximity to the beach—was immediately available at a price that was not outrageous. The beach house in St. James turned out to be perfect. We worked at our desks starting in the early morning. Before lunch, we luxuriated for an hour or two in the sun and the caressing Caribbean Sea that regaled us with an unending fashion show of fish darting about the coral reef, and then went home for lunch and the postprandial nap that was our moment of choice for making love. Afterward, until late in the evening, we worked again. After a week of this paradisal existence, Bella told me, as we were leaving the lunch table, that for once we would have to rest quietly during our nap. She hurt everywhere and, it seemed to her, particularly down there. She had noticed some strange bleeding. Would I mind? Immediately, I told her that we must book seats on the next available flight to New York and see our family doctor and whomever else he thought appropriate. She refused categorically, insisting that we stay on the island through the remaining two weeks of our lease. There was no reason to sacrifice even one moment of our idyll. It didn't take long, however, after we returned to the city to learn that there had been reasons aplenty. Bella's symptoms were those of acute lymphoblastic leukemia that had attacked her bone marrow and was methodically, implacably subverting it. Increasingly draconic treatments would be followed by perhaps a month's remission. The cycle was repeated over and over, leaving Bella ravaged and exhausted, with no hope of cure or longer-lasting remission, according to her hematologist, other than a successful bone marrow transplant. Bella's only sibling, her older brother, was eager to be the donor. The consanguinity and the resulting near-perfect match of their blood types reduced considerably the risk of rejection. After considering the protocol she would be required to observe following the transplant, and the benefits she could expect, about which she was stubbornly skeptical, Bella decided against the procedure. I don't believe this cancer will leave my body, and I don't care about gaining a couple of years, she said. They won't be good years. We've had such a splendid life together. Let's not settle for one in which I will be so horribly diminished. Neither of us wants that. There was no hiding of the fact that I agreed. With the help of opiates we had saved up she died in my arms, peacefully, some six months later. And what can be said of me? I am on a rack, but I still have my work. I do it conscientiously and modestly for the pleasure it gives me, expecting no other award. And I have my memories. Dante's Virgil was wrong to tell him that there is no greater sorrow than to remember past happy times when one is in misery. Memory is a solace. Perhaps the only one. Memory is also the best of companions.

My reverie was interrupted by a voice I knew, although I didn't immediately identify it, calling out my name: Philip! I turned and saw a tall slim lady in her late sixties or perhaps early seventies, strikingly good looking and turned out in a black suit I attributed to Armani and black pumps. A black pocketbook hung from her shoulder on a gold chain. I blinked as I realized who she was. Many years had passed since I had last seen her. How many I couldn't immediately calculate. But yes, without doubt, it was she.

My goodness, the lady continued, what's the matter with you, don't you know me? I knew you right away, even with your back turned. Your hair is all white, it's still cut too short, and your ears still stick out. I had no idea I'd changed so much. For God's sake, I'm Lucy Snow. Lucy De Bourgh Snow.

Yielding to irritation because her voice had been much louder than necessary, I replied using Hubert H. Humphrey's standard response to strangers who introduced themselves while he pumped their hands: Of course you are, and I'm glad to see you.

Well, I should hope so!

This was said somewhat sternly.

What are you doing here? she continued. I thought you'd given up on New York.

Not in the least, I told her. I've been away a good deal, but I've never stopped being a New Yorker. This time I've come home to stay.

That's good news, she said, we will reconnect.

In rapid order she went on to inform me that she was living in the city but since she still had her place in Little Compton was able to keep one foot in Rhode Island; that both her parents were dead, as was her sister-in-law Edie; that her brother John hadn't remarried, was living in the big house in Bristol, and took even more seriously than their parents its significance in the history of the state; and that there were many things to catch up about. Thereupon we heard the gong summoning us to our seats. As we separated—she was in the mezzanine and I in the orchestra—she announced she'd look for me at the next intermission.

I made a sincere effort to pay attention to the goings-on onstage—a Balanchine ballet that was not one of my favorites—but it was no use. I couldn't stop my mind from wandering. Good heavens, Lucy! I wasn't sure that I had seen her more than once or twice after her and Thomas's divorce, and that would have been in the late seventies. Possibly in the early eighties. In fact, it seemed likely that the only times I had given her any thought must have been when I saw Thomas, alone or with his new wife, which I had done with some frequency, and inevitably when I read Thomas's obituary. Other than the obituary, it all seemed desperately long ago. Lucy could have been one of those Radcliffe, Smith, or Vassar girls of good family who came to New York in the 1950s after college in search of a husband or the dream job. You met them at a cocktail party given by somebody's aunt or godmother. They were mostly attractive—Lucy had been, depending on the angle from which you saw her, a great beauty or a *jolie laide*—and if conjugal bliss and raising the perfect family in Bronxville, Scarsdale, or Morristown was not their principal immediate object, they wanted to write. In the meantime, they were looking for a job in book publishing or at *Time, LIFE,* or the *Saturday Evening Post.* Unfortunately, the men who dispensed such jobs thought that girls of their sort were best suited to answering the phone and bringing coffee. A good way to break out of the stereotype and escape was to go to work instead for a fashion magazine. That's what Lucy did. A couple of years after Sylvia Plath's stint there, she competed successfully for a summer job as guest editor at *Mademoiselle,* went back to Radcliffe for her senior year, and after graduation proved once again clever or lucky. She wangled a year's internship at the Paris *Vogue,* a posting that must have made the aspiring writers and journalists among her classmates break out in hives from envy.

Lucy was apparently special in other ways as well—at least in the context of the early 1950s. A man I played squash with twice a week, at the Harvard Club when I invited and at his grand Park Avenue club when it was his turn, had remained a regular on the debutante party circuit. He had been at the ball the De Bourghs gave for Lucy at their mansion the summer before she started at Radcliffe and had kept up with her during the New York season that followed, at the Junior Assemblies and every other conceivable venue, apparently including some he didn't care to specify. She was ravishing, a knockout, he told me, she electrified every stag line and would have easily been the debutante of the year if it hadn't been for rumors about the unfortunate business at Miss Porter's just as she was due to graduate. She'd gone AWOL—according to the account he'd heard she'd shimmied down a rope from her dormitory window—and was discovered sleeping off a bender at a Howard Johnson's outside Farmington. Her swain had already departed, and she refused to reveal his name to the police or the headmistress or even her parents. Mr. De Bourgh pulled strings and wrote a big check so that she was allowed to graduate, and he and Mrs. De Bourgh went ahead with the party. Whether they held their noses was an open question, since the invitations had been sent out and it would have been a bigger embarrassment to cancel. My squash partner made these revelations as we rested in his club's locker room after an arduous match. In keeping with the atmosphere of the place, he added a personal testimonial: She fucks like a maenad. A snooty maenad!

Paris was where I got to know her well. At first we'd only run into each other at American embassy functions. Ambassador Dillon and his successor, Amory Houghton, had been at school with her father; they made a point of looking after her. Later she began to invite me to the elegant little dinner parties she gave at her apartment on rue Casimir-Perier, a short walk from place du Palais Bourbon, where *Vogue* had its office at the time. Then one thing led to another. There were many young American students and expats in Paris at the time. The strong dollar made luxuries affordable. Lunch for two at Lapérouse, with a decent bottle of wine, set one back, after a generous tip, perhaps twelve dollars. The war in Algeria had not yet heated up, and the lure of the intellectual and literary life in Paris was at a zenith, stoked by the reputations and powerful personalities of Sartre, Simone de Beauvoir, and Camus, as well as the vogue for existentialism and French cinema. Lucy stood out among the Americans of her age. As is well known, the very rich are different from the rest of us: they possess and enjoy early and are convinced that they are better than we. Lucy wasn't very rich herself, but the aura of historical importance and wealth that surrounded her was unmistakable. Her forebears, the eighteenth-century De Bourghs, had been well-to-do ship owners in Bristol, Rhode Island. The one who was her direct ancestor, James De Bourgh, had commanded a ship before he was twenty; during the War of 1812 he was a dreaded privateer on the American side; after a career in Rhode Island state politics he became a U.S. senator. His huge fortune, consolidated through cotton manufacturing, had been earned in the slave trade; when he died in the late 1830s he was said to be the richest man in Rhode Island and possibly the second-richest man in the country. I suppose it was John Jacob Astor who beat him out for the first place, but I've never taken the trouble to confirm my hunch. Although by the time I met Lucy, the De Bourgh saga was hardly known to anyone who wasn't an American history buff, and even I, who qualified as such, had initially had only a sketchy recollection that there had once existed an important De Bourgh, I had perforce become familiar with it. One simply couldn't spend much time with Lucy and not hear about James De Bourgh and his Rhode Island contemporaries and rivals, the far-better-known brothers John and Moses Brown. She inveighed against the gradual frittering away of the De Bourgh fortune under the stewardship of James's descendants, among the more feckless of whom she counted her own father, and American trade policies she blamed for the collapse of New England textile mills in the 1920s, which her grandfather and his brothers had failed to anticipate, but so far as she was concerned her family's glow had not been diminished.

Besides, as she used to say, losing your shirt is a relative concept. Everything depends on how many shirts you have left. We've still got many to go.

She astonished me by turning down the junior editor's job in New York that the magazine offered her at the end of the internship. Living in New York, she said, wasn't for her. Instead, she went home for the summer in order to get in some good tennis, she said, and in the fall returned to Paris, her apartment, and her dinner parties. After one of them, while we were having a nightcap, I asked what she planned to do now that she was back.

To live! she answered breezily. To dare to live!

She expatiated on that concept in the course of subsequent conversations. Wasn't she an heiress of all the ages, duty bound to take full advantage of her education—she had a comically high opinion of her Radcliffe degree in Romance languages and literature—and above all her freedom? Family trusts, though hardly as ample as they might once have been, allowed her to carry on the way she did. Why take a job she didn't need or particularly want and, coincidentally, deprive someone to whom it might make a real difference?

I had no ready answer other than "of course," although I wondered how well she had pondered the fate of nineteenth-century expatriated ladies on whom consciously or not she might be modeling herself. Besides, it wasn't any of my business. Lucy and I got along well, and having her in Paris organizing her dinners and occasionally more ambitious entertainments was pleasant. A case in point was an expedition to Chartres with her and a married couple from Providence on their honeymoon in France. Talking nonstop about the architecture of the cathedral and Henry Adams's take on it, she barreled down the three-lane *route nationale,* which the shadows cast by plane trees lining it on both sides had turned into the semblance of a shimmering stream, her four-door Mercedes convertible leaving in the dust the *deux chevaux* carrying the humbler French and the big sleek Citroëns beloved of French bourgeoisie and government officials, until the gendarmes stopped us at a speed trap about thirty kilometers from our destination. They were polite, and so was she, but, as she said when we resumed our journey, some of the squeak had gone out of her. But only for that morning. By the afternoon we had her in fighting trim again, and the trip back to Paris was even more hair-raising. Her theory was that cops never stop you twice on the same road. Besides, she had a dinner date, and she didn't want to be late.

As the intermission approached, it occurred to me that I had enough stored-up memories and enough living ghosts—former persons, I called them—encircling me, school and college classmates, people I had worked with at one journal or another, and my literary agent to whom I had remained faithful, and had no need to add Lucy to the crowd. The thing to do might be to stay in my seat during the intermission. Alternatively, I could skip the third piece on the program, a Balanchine ballet I had seen too often to care about missing it, leave the theater, and go directly to dinner. The conscience of a balletomane prevailed. There was no good reason to avoid Lucy, and certainly none to let her drive me away.

Lucy must have turned to see which way I was going when we parted after the first intermission. She was waiting for me at the top of the stairs.

Well, she said, that was fine dancing. Did you enjoy it?

I nodded.

There may be better dancers in Europe, she continued, I wouldn't know. I don't go to Europe anymore. But to my mind this company is still wonderful.

I assured her that I agreed, whereupon she asked, Aren't you going to offer me a glass of champagne?

It turned out she wanted mixed nuts as well. I paid and followed her out to the balcony. There she told me with scarcely a pause between sentences that she had been sorry to read about Bella and should have written, but she hadn't known her very well, and that she supposed losing her had made me very lonely.

Shocked by the callousness of her remarks, I turned toward the fountain and remained silent.

After a pause she said she remembered that I, on the other hand, had written after Thomas died, which she thought then and continued to think had been a gesture of misguided politeness. Not expecting condolences, she hadn't answered.

I may have shrugged before replying that I had liked Thomas and had regretted their divorce when I heard about it, as well as, of course, the ghastly accident.

She turned on me.

What do you mean! I couldn't have gone on living with that monster. You went on seeing him, of course, just like all the rest of my friends. Yup, everything he wanted fell into his lap, including that celebrity second wife, and he never acknowledged that he owed it all to me. Perhaps he didn't remember. Perhaps he never got it.

I didn't bother to reply.

My son, Jamie, is a failure, she added inconsequentially. He tries to write screenplays but doesn't know how. No wonder he can't sell them. His wife is a Chicana. Naturally they live in a creepy suburb of L.A. When I go out there, he doesn't even let me stay in his house. I have to go to a motel!

That's hard, I said.

This time she agreed. Their story is that Thomas never asked to stay with them. Naturally! Why would he have? He stayed in a suite at the Beverly Hills Hotel and had himself driven out and back! You know that he had absolutely no sense of direction.

I couldn't help laughing. He may have well chosen the better solution, I told her.

Certainly, she replied, he could afford it.

She must have realized that I was about to say goodbye and changed the subject: I suppose you're meeting people for dinner. You can tell the truth. I've already eaten, so you don't have to worry about whether I'll fit in. I eat early these days. Some other evening, though, I'd like to have you over for dinner. What's your telephone number?

I gave it to her, together with my e-mail address.

She wrote both down in a dog-eared address book and said, I'll be in touch.

II

THOMAS SNOW: the brilliant investment banker who made a pile of money, gave much of it away, and turned into a Wall Street pundit! We had enjoyed getting together wherever I lived, in New York or Paris, and beginning in the late seventies he came through Paris often. Of course I had followed him on various op-ed pages in U.S. newspapers and occasionally in the *Financial Times*. Lucy's speaking of him with such hostility and resentment, which apparently time had done nothing to assuage, brought back before my eyes the young man she introduced to me one afternoon in Paris, some fifty years ago. I was in my study, working on the first chapter of a novel, which in my case meant that I was revising perhaps for the third or fourth time whatever I had written the day before. The telephone rang; I picked up the receiver and heard Lucy speaking very loudly: Hello, I'm practically downstairs from you, at the café on the corner of Vaugirard and Madame. I've got someone with me I want you to meet. May we come up? We won't stay long.

She was one of those people, convinced that you cannot fail to recognize their voice, who don't give their name when they call. In the event I had realized it was she and repressed my annoyance. Since saying no and feeling badly about it would have been more disruptive, I said, Yes, I'll be glad to see you.

I lived on the third floor, French style, which is really the fourth floor. There was no elevator. A few long minutes passed before the doorbell rang. I opened the door. The look on Lucy's face was that of a cat bringing you a mouse. She pushed forward a boyish American and said: This is Thomas Snow. Thomas, here is the great novelist I've been telling you about.

We shook hands. It was after six, and he was so obviously embarrassed by her introduction that, contrary to my original intention to get rid of them quickly, I showed them into the living room and asked whether they would like a drink. The whiskey relaxed the young man. A casual question about what had brought him to Paris in January, not a month favored by tourists, opened the sluice gate to a flood of information. He was a GI on leave. Having gotten his master's from the London School of Economics, where he had gone on a Harvard College fellowship, he volunteered for the draft and was serving as a corporal with the Seventh Army headquarters in Heidelberg. His tour of duty would be over in the summer. In the fall, he'd start at the Harvard Business School.

And afterward?

He had it all mapped out: he wanted to work on Wall Street and had his eye on Morgan Stanley and, if that didn't work out, Kidder. Beyond that, he had dreams, some more nebulous than others.

That's quite a program, I said, and turning to Lucy asked where she had met this remarkable future banker.

But I was going to tell you about it, I was just getting to that, Thomas protested. We met at the beginning of the second semester of my senior year, at a party given by your good friend Alex van Buren. I know that you and he are friends because Lucy has told me. It was an extraordinary stroke of luck. She and I hit it off right away. I can't imagine how we would have met otherwise.

Lucy nodded vigorously and held out her glass, which I refilled.

How interesting, I said. What was Alex doing in Cambridge? He graduated years ago. Ahead of me.

He'd been working at the family brokerage firm, Thomas explained, and the decision was made that he should go to the business school. His father pushed for it.

Actually, Lucy had gotten it slightly wrong. I had known Alex, we had been on good terms, he'd always been very nice to me, but we had never been close. A few years older than I, he had been in the marines and managed to survive Iwo Jima. We had overlapped briefly at the *Lampoon;* in fact he'd helped me get in, but that was all. I supposed he went to *Lampoon* dinners. I didn't. Remembering the conspicuously rich and snobby New Yorkers he'd hung out with, I had to wonder what on earth this young man had been doing at one of Alex's parties. There was no need to probe: the explanation was forthcoming. It looked as though Thomas had decided to tell me his life story, and Lucy seemed content to let him talk, maternally proud of his polite self-assurance.

He had gotten to know Alex and Alex's parents, Thomas continued, indeed the entire van Buren clan, over the summers he spent, since his junior year in high school, babysitting and tutoring the van Buren nieces, nephews, and grandchildren in math and history at the family's summer place in Newport. He was from Newport himself, but not the van Burens' kind of Newport—the notion that I might think otherwise made him shake with laughter. His father owned the garage where everybody, the van Burens included, had their fancy cars serviced, and his mother was a bookkeeper. She's my father's business manager. I'm an only child, he added.

Then you've grown up near Bristol, I observed, De Bourgh territory.

He laughed. Yes, a short distance as the crow flies! But otherwise . . . Anyway, the summer before Alex went to the business school he told me he'd be in touch once he had settled down in Cambridge. Being a really good guy, he did call and invite me to parties he and his roommate gave after football games. Then in February of my senior year he invited me, out of the blue, to a small party without a theme. Just those deadly martinis. By the pitcher. She was there—he smiled in the direction of Lucy—and right away he introduced me. I'll say it again. He's a really great guy. I don't mean just the war-hero stuff. You know he has a Silver Star with three clusters and two Purple Hearts. I mean, he's never treated me like an employee, nothing remotely like it. He taught me sailing, talked to me for hours about the First World War, which was then my big subject. He reads a lot of history.

That was nice to hear. The decorations were news to me. They showed a modesty that Alex in fact had shared with some of the other returning veterans I got to know at college. You never heard about the Iwo Jima horrors or the Battle of the Bulge or whatever else they had lived through. The generosity toward this young man was mildly surprising; perhaps Alex had turned over a new leaf. But as Thomas talked on about the van Burens' estate and his wide-eyed astonishment at the tennis court, the near-Olympic-length swimming pool, the boathouse with its sculls and sailing paraphernalia, the kids' dinghies swinging at their moorings, and the yawl belonging to Alex's father on which he and Mrs. van Buren would take him and his charges for day sails, I wondered whether he had already seen the De Bourgh establishment or realized that it was in all likelihood no less grand. He wasn't telling, but he surely knew he was not the sort of young beau Lucy's friends would expect her to be taking around and introducing to them. In fact, I was willing to bet that his stream of true confessions was intended to make clear he understood such surprise as I felt and had no intention of fooling anyone about his background. He needn't have worried about that. You couldn't pull the wool over the eyes of people who were of Lucy's world and cared about such matters. Yes, he was trim—I learned later that he had been on his high school track team and had specialized in the one-hundred- and two-hundred-meter dash—and respectably taller than she, he had brown hair parted on the side and a nice face with regular features, and he wore a gray-flannel Brooks Brothers suit that was neither too big nor too small for him and a blue button-down shirt just like everybody else's. If Norman Rockwell had wanted to put on a *Saturday Evening Post* cover a bright-eyed GI on leave, out on a first date with his future boss's daughter, he might have used this kid—jazzed up a bit of course. And yes, he spoke correctly and without a trace of a regional accent. That was fine and should go down well with his prospective white-shoe Wall Street employers. But in the De Bourgh context, it was no use. He was a townie. The son of a garage owner and a bookkeeper! That might not have mattered much if the garage— the best in town!—had been, say, in Casper, Wyoming. But the indignity of its being next door, in Newport, of all places, was hilarious and bound to give the De Bourgh parents and Lucy's brother, and I didn't know how many uncles, aunts, and cousins, a lasting heartburn. That last aspect of the matter, incidentally, turned out to be something I got mostly wrong. Beyond such divagations about class and caste on the Eastern Seaboard of the United States, which were part of my writer's métier, there was another oddity: there were many bankers and lawyers in Lucy's milieu in Paris, most of them, to be sure, safely married, but I hadn't noticed that Lucy was particularly interested in any of them. She played tennis doubles with them and their wives; she went to their parties and dinners; she seemed drawn, however, to the other group of Americans in Paris: writers, painters, and occasional journalists. So why this embryo banker? It wasn't any of my business. If Lucy had a thing going with this nice boy, *tant mieux!* He was likely to have a good time and learn a thing or two. I liked him instinctively, and I liked the conceit I'd come up with, that in fine, to use one of the Master's locutions, all three of us, Lucy, Thomas, and I, belonged to the same world, undifferentiated by class, the grand world to which presidents of Harvard University traditionally welcomed at commencements graduating Harvard College seniors: "the society of educated men and women." Buoyed by these sentiments, I asked Thomas and Lucy to come to a little cocktail party I was giving at my apartment on Friday of that same week.

I had been living long enough in Paris to become friends with an interesting group of French literary and artistic types, whom I was sure Lucy would like, including a couple of fine music and art critics—and had invited a number of them, as well as some Americans working for the *New York Times,* the *Herald Tribune,* and *Time.* The French and the Americans didn't make much of an effort to mix, but that was par for the course. I kept an eye on Thomas. At first he remained at Lucy's side, but eventually American journalists who crowded to speak to her in effect shoved him aside. I was about to go to his rescue when I saw that no intervention was needed. He was chatting away with Guy Seurat, the great-grandson of the postimpressionist painter and my best friend in France. I joined them briefly and found Thomas's French a bit stiff but perfectly sufficient. When I next checked,

Guy was introducing him to an editor at Gallimard and his Sorbonne-professor wife. It was a good thing, I thought, that he had connected with the French contingent. Several of the American guests had a history with Lucy. There was no way Thomas could have known that, unless she had chosen to tell him, but such things can sometimes be inferred from the way a man takes your measure, and they hurt.

Sometime before summer I ran into Lucy at a reception at the British embassy. It was a beautiful mild evening. We left at the same time, and when she told me she was going home, I suggested that we walk together. I would leave her at her door and continue to rue de Vaugirard. There is no greater or more exhilarating public space or urban view than that offered by the astonishing ensemble of place de la Concorde, the bridge that crosses the Seine and takes you to the National Assembly, and the vista of Notre-Dame to the east and Pont Alexandre III and the Trocadéro to the west. For a while we savored it in silence. Then she told me that she and Thomas would tour Italy together as soon as he had finished his army service. Her brother was getting married in Bristol on the second Saturday of September. Of course, she'd be there. After the wedding, she'd probably return to Paris. She hoped I'd be there.

I observed that it seemed as though she and that very nice Thomas had something serious going.

He really loves me, she answered. I think he needs me. Perhaps I need him too.

.   .   .

A novel of mine was published in the United States in February of the following year, making it necessary for me to go to New York to see my editor and various public relations people at the publishing house, as well as my agent, and do some readings and other promotional events. It was good to get away from Paris. The conflict over the future of Algeria was tearing France apart with a vehemence not known since the Dreyfus Affair. Toward the end of my stay, invited by the Harvard College literary magazine, I gave a talk at the Sanders Theater in Cambridge. The turnout was good, and the audience agreeably enthusiastic. Unbeknownst to me, Thomas had come to hear me and waited to say hello as I left the building on the way to a reception the undergraduates were giving at the magazine. I invited him to come along. On our way to Bow Street, he gave me an enthusiastic, even bubbly, account of his and Lucy's Italian tour. They had "done" Florence and the Umbrian towns, Venice, Padua, and Rome and then, after a two-day visit to Naples, drove back to Paris, where they parted. He took the train to Le Havre, from which his student ship was sailing. She was due to sail a week later, from Cherbourg. First-class on the *France,* he told me. Lucky Lucy! But they got back together in Bristol, at her brother's wedding. Then she left for Paris and Geneva.

I asked what news he had from her.

She's still in Geneva, he told me. I've been getting letters, but we've only spoken a couple of times. The difference in time zones seems to get in the way. She didn't come home for Christmas. I'm worried about her. She's never explained what she's doing there. If I can swing it, I'll go over right after school ends. I'll have too much work to do it over the spring break.

In May of that year, not long after my return to Paris, my friend Guy Seurat and his doctor wife, Elsa, invited me to spend the long Ascension weekend with them at their house in the Vaucluse, a couple kilometers from the little town of Camaret-sur-Aigues. Standing in a large garden, it had been in Guy's family until the 1880s, when it passed into the hands of a rich industrialist from Marseilles and his heirs, who had inflicted on it the sort of improvements that have defaced so many similar French residences. The family bought back the property in the 1930s, and Guy, ever since he inherited it from a bachelor uncle, had been engaged in a heroic and not-inexpensive effort to restore its exterior, including removing the modern stucco and replacing it with a *crépi*—slaked-lime plaster—of a color typical of the region. He and Elsa did much of the work themselves, enlisting friends whenever they could, and I had myself spent one Easter vacation sanding and painting window shutters and uprooting grass from the front courtyard so that it could be replaced, in the eighteenth-century manner, by fine gravel.

When I arrived by car from Avignon in the late afternoon, Guy and Elsa's other guests were already there, a couple I didn't know: a black-haired, pale-complexioned young woman of stunning beauty and a large man dressed in an outfit—lime linen slacks and a red silk shirt worn with a silk paisley ascot—that his kind of French bourgeois considered appropriate for weekends in the country and shopped for at Sulka's on rue de Castiglione. They were, I learned moments later, Bella and her husband Marc de Clam. Ascension was late that year, and a dry very warm day was followed by the sort of Provençal night that makes you wish dawn would never come. A late dinner was served on a trestle table under a moonless sky by the Seurats' combination housekeeper and cook, who together with her husband also watched over the property in the Seurats' absence, a not-inconsiderable responsibility in a part of the country plagued by burglaries. I found myself seated next to Marc. He talked volubly. The failed Generals' Putsch, an attempt by disaffected high-ranking officers to overthrow General de Gaulle, had taken place a mere three weeks ago; and OAS, the clandestine arm of Algérie Française, the Algeria-must-remain-French movement, had begun its campaign of assassinations and violence. His sympathies clearly lay, if not with OAS itself, then with the *pieds-noirs,* the non-Muslim population of Algeria in part descended from French colonists, who refused to give up the country they considered theirs. My views were diametrically opposed to Algérie Française and everything it stood for, but I didn't contradict him. Nor did I ask what kind of link of ancestry there was between him and Armand du Paty de Clam, who would have surely approved of his tirade. I hardly spoke. My thoughts and gaze were fixed on Bella; it was a *coup de foudre:* lightning had struck, I had fallen in love.

Dinner ended very late. Another couple, Bernard and

Francine Bruneau, had joined us. The housekeeper had gone to bed, so we all cleared the table and scraped and rinsed the dishes before stacking them in the sink and on the kitchen table. As I watched the Clam couple say good night and disappear, I was gripped by envy, precise and humiliating. Guy proposed an after-dinner scotch. I accepted. After some hesitation Bernard and Francine said they too were going to bed. It was what I had hoped for: I was left alone with Guy and Elsa. When the conversation became desultory, I asked them about the other guests.

It's a class reunion! cried Elsa. All three of them were at Stan all the way through *hypokhâgne*. And then Bernard and Marc were together again at Sciences Po.

Bernard is in business with his father, who is an antique dealer on Faubourg St.-Honoré, she continued, and Marc works for Banque Worms.

I had frequented enough members of the elegant Parisian bourgeoisie to know that by Stan they meant Collège Stanislas, the most esteemed of French Catholic schools among whose eminent graduates was none other than General de Gaulle, so detested by Marc de Clam.

And the wives? I asked.

Francine has twin boys. She left them with the grandparents for the weekend. That's a job and a half, but she also helps out in the antiques business. She did the École du Louvre.

And Bella, Guy chimed in, the redoubtable Bella! She went through *khâgne* at Fénelon and came in second or third in the examination for Normale Sup. Of course she got in and graduated brilliantly. Midway through Normale, she married Marc. She's never taught. Instead, she's one of my authors. Two years ago we published her delectable little study of Madame de La Fayette. She's working on something new now, but she won't say what.

"Redoubtable"! I thought I had sensed it: she was as brainy as she was beautiful. Fénelon was the best of girls' lycées; École Normale Supérieure was the *nec plus ultra* of French humanities education. The intellectual snob inside me was smiling and nodding approval.

Your pal Marc has some strong political opinions, I ventured. Is she onboard with them?

Guy laughed. Certainly not! She's a closet socialist. She doesn't pay attention to his politics. None of us do. He's a special French product: the lovable right-wing nut.

Elsa chimed in: He has it in his genes. You should hear him on the subject of that traitor Dreyfus!

We remained silent for a while, gazing at the stars that were so bright one truly believed they were burning. When Guy stretched and said good night, Elsa told him she'd be right up and asked whether I would like another whiskey. A small one, I told her. She poured it and poured one for herself.

It's been a tough week, she said. It's my turn to be responsible for the emergency room, and we've had a record load of trauma cases. Car crashes, knife and bullet wounds, plus the usual heart attacks, strokes, kids falling off bicycles on their heads. You may have sensed it, she continued, abruptly changing the subject. It's not a good marriage. Bella does her best. There are no children; I have a feeling there won't be any, and it's just a question of when she will decide she's had enough. If you can believe it, Marc resents her writing. He claims it makes his colleagues and clients nervous!

The next day Bernard Bruneau organized an antiques-hunting expedition to Nîmes and Arles. There was general enthusiasm for the project, Bernard and Elsa being adepts of flea markets and provincial dealers, as was apparently Marc de Clam. I begged off. The day was gorgeous and less hot than the day before, and it seemed a pity to spend most of it in a car being driven too fast on the murderous D15. It occurred to me that I should instead get into my own car, head at a reasonable speed in the direction of Uzès, and take a long walk in the *garrigue*. The mere thought of the aroma of sunbaked juniper, wild thyme, and lavender was intoxicating. I announced my plan and held to it despite expressions of regret and promises to go on a hike the next day and the day after. To my surprise and delight, Bella asked if she could join me.

It turned out that she had read one of my novels and remembered it well. We talked about my themes. They were, I said, though not necessarily in that order, love and ambition and betrayal and fear of the ravages of old age. Told through events transpiring in New York and New England, with occasional forays by my personages to places I knew best in Western Europe. She smiled and said there were no other serious themes, except perhaps death itself and retribution and forgiveness. I agreed. Retribution could be found tucked in my work. Forgiveness? It was a subject that had seldom engaged my attention.

We came to a spot where I could safely park the car, got out, and made our way through the scrub. Soon we were in the open, surrounded by a sea of low vegetation alive with chirruping crickets and inhaling the rich smells I had remembered with such longing.

This is pure heaven, said Bella. I am so happy you thought of doing this and let me come along.

My reply was going to be some meaningless compliment, but, suddenly emboldened, I told her that Guy had mentioned publishing her book—which I regretted not having read but would read in Paris—and a new book she was writing. Would she tell me the subject?

I've only done preliminary research, she said, but I think I'll keep going and probably write something. It's about an unusual moment in the history of the émigrés who fled the Reign of Terror. The time spent in the United States by Chateaubriand and Talleyrand, who did not stay for long but saw a great deal and wrote down their impressions, and by Marquise de la Tour du Pin, whose memoirs are wonderful. In Chateaubriand's case, of course, we owe to that voyage *Atala* and *Les Natchez*.

Those were works I had read, I told her, and had some idea of their influence. I also said, trying to be as modest as possible and at the same time invite her interest, that shortly after college, when I began to think about my first book, I steeped myself for a while in late eighteenth-century American history; I had been particularly interested in what was going on in New England and New York.

Then we must have lunch in Paris, she said, if you ever have time. I would like so much to test some of my theories—no, they're not quite that. They're only some assumptions.

III

THE MISSION in Iraq having been "accomplished," I had half seriously allowed myself to suppose that the next step in that poor country's 2003 march toward happiness and democracy would include the early restoration to Iraqis of self-rule. Instead, the morning after the ballet I saw on the front page of the *NYT* a photo of our proconsul in Baghdad, Paul Bremer, and his predecessor Jay Garner looking as though they had each swallowed a particularly pungent meatball, and an article to the effect that the United States and Great Britain had decided to delay self-rule. Allied officials—presumably Mr. Bremer—would remain in charge indefinitely. The telephone rang as I was pondering the implications of that high-handed move. It was Lucy, calling to invite me to dinner that very evening. She said she was still at the Park Avenue address. Dinner was at eight. The weather having continued to be unusually mild, I decided to walk there and crossed the park at Seventy-Ninth

Street. Eighth floor, the doorman told me. She's expecting you. The door is open.

The apartment was as I recalled it from my first visit, soon after Thomas and Lucy came to live in the city: large, with a profusion of fine early nineteenth-century American furniture, rather-less-good portraits of unsmiling men, women, and family groups who had to be ancestors, because why else would one display them in one's house, and beautiful Oriental rugs. I had assumed, and saw no reason now to change my view, that it all came from Lucy's family. Although at the time of my first visit her parents were both alive and presumably intended that the big house in Bristol and everything of importance in it should go to her older brother John, she had probably been left all sorts of things by her De Bourgh and Goddard grandparents. After all, she was the only granddaughter. I could also imagine a barn or, given the quality of this stuff, more likely a warehouse, where those two families of slavers turned industrialists stored unneeded furniture, paintings, table silver, and linen to be drawn upon as needed in order to furnish homes of younger sons and daughters. Lucy had at the time of that first visit given me a rapid tour, pointing out the improvements she and Thomas had made after decades of neglect by the bedridden previous owner. When we returned to the library, Thomas was there, having just returned from the office, and offered drinks—a whiskey for her and martinis poured out of a cut-crystal shaker for him and me. I congratulated them on their elegant, indeed luxurious, installation. Lucy shook her head rebelliously, a gesture I remembered as typical when she was going to contradict you and felt strongly about it.

The location isn't all that good, she said. Many people one knows consider being even a couple of blocks north of Seventy-Second Street unacceptable as a matter of principle.

I raised my eyebrows at that.

No need to make funny faces, she told me. We're also on the wrong side of Park Avenue. The good buildings are on the other side and get the morning sun. We had to settle for second best not because I wanted to but because my trustee wouldn't give me one penny more. Just in case you have any doubts about it, that's where the money comes from. My trust! If we were trying to make do on what Thomas makes at Kidder we'd be living in Harlem or Hoboken and I doubt you'd be visiting us!

I thought it odd that Thomas hadn't gotten the job with Morgan Stanley he had hoped for. A moment later, he explained. Kidder had always been his second choice, but it moved to first place when Al Gordon, the head of the firm and a great man, came to Cambridge to recruit him personally and made clear that he and Thomas would be working closely together.

Lucy's vision of what their existence would be if they had had to depend on Thomas's salary struck me as peculiarly noir. I supposed that all good investment banks paid their young people pretty much the same, and yet my cousin Josiah Weld, who had gone to work for Morgan Stanley and was Thomas's exact contemporary, didn't seem to live in dire misery. In fact, Josiah's mother had recently told me how much he earned. It was a modest amount but hardly coolie wages, and when a week earlier I had gone to drinks with Josiah and his wife, Molly, at their apartment on Central Park West and Ninety-Third Street, I hadn't had the impression that I was slumming—even if it wasn't Park Avenue, north of Seventy-Second Street! It so happened that the conversation at the Welds' had turned to how young people were getting by in New York—Josiah's classmates who, for example, were also investment bankers or lawyers and, like him, had very little money of their own or received minimal help from their families. According to Molly, those who already had children lived in more-or-less-rundown middle-class apartment buildings on the upper reaches of West End Avenue or even on West 106th Street. Lower-middle-class, Josiah corrected her. There wouldn't be enough bedrooms, she went on, but one could manage. The big problem if you were way uptown was coming home at night. One had to be very careful. That is why, Molly concluded, they had decided to wait a couple of years before they had children. The picture the Welds had given me had seemed on the whole reasonable; it was pretty much what I had expected.

As for Lucy and Thomas's spread, it put them in a different league. A Kidder partner, perhaps even Mr. Gordon himself, would have felt quite comfortable ensconced in their apartment. I had a fleeting feeling that the apartment and everything about it spelled trouble. The expense would remain beyond Thomas's ability to sustain for several years, even if his ascent to partnership was prompt. That meant that Lucy had better be prepared to pay up and be nice about it. I could imagine the envy, if not ill will, of colleagues who didn't have a trust like Lucy's to fall back on. As for the effect on Thomas's mother and father and aunts, uncles, and cousins, assuming any of them were invited to visit, I couldn't even speculate about it. An unpleasant corollary might be the collectively raised eyebrows of the De Bourgh clan when they surveyed the posh surroundings in which their family fortune had installed the son of the garage owner from Newport who'd been getting the kinks out of their friends' Jaguars and Bentleys. Would it be the sense of God-fearing satisfaction, because money earned selling human cargoes had been put to virtuous use, giving a promising young man of humble origin a good start? Benign amusement or indignation? Lucy's own De Bourgh feelings lay just below the surface. I feared that they were unlikely to be simple.

I shook myself free of these memories. Forty years or so older than the young *maîtresse de la maison* I had been brooding about, Lucy came into the room and offered me her cheek to kiss. The old Lucy had smelled of L'Heure Bleue and sandalwood soap, her other Guerlain favorite. The new version smelled ever so slightly of mothballs—had the white cashmere she wore been put away for the summer and insufficiently aired out before she put it on?—and if you were close to her when she spoke, as I was to be when she offered me her cheek to kiss, of something sour. Perhaps it was dryness of the mouth.

Well, well, well, she said, so you've actually come!

Was there any doubt? I replied. I did accept your invitation.

Ah yes, but the other evening at the ballet you were less than thrilled to see me. An unglamorous ghost from your past who's inviting you to dinner alone because she hasn't any glamorous guests she could round up to amuse you. Of course, I didn't let that thought stop me, but I fully expected an e-mail saying you were sick or had to leave town or God knows what other fib. E-mails make lying easy.

Seeing that I was about to protest, she added, Never mind, we've time to talk about that later. What would you like to drink?

I wondered whether she had guessed how close she had come to the mark. The temptation to let her know that I was paralyzed by an accumulation of work and to promise to be in touch as soon as the crisis was over had been powerful. What had stopped me? In part it was a peculiar new form of piety, the sense that I owed it as a propitiatory offering to my dead, more numerous now than the living for whom I had any affection, to be considerate and indulgent even with tiresome acquaintances, and friends who had become nothing more than tiresome acquaintances, as well as with less-than-satisfactory housekeepers, cleaning ladies, typists, personal assistants, accountants, doctors, dentists, and barbers and perhaps even my literary agent and my editor. A more potent reason was that our chance encounter at the ballet brought back memories of a time in Paris that I had long ago put out of my mind. Among them was that of Lucy's and my *passade,* which predated by more than a year the afternoon when she brought Thomas to see me. It gave her certain inalienable rights. The setting had been a house party over a three-day spring weekend in a large villa that the partner in charge of the Paris office of a New York law firm had rented outside Deauville. A band of Americans, some of whom I knew, had been invited. Lucy was among them. On Saturday evening there was a lot of drinking, and after dinner we danced to records. Somebody dimmed the lights. I soon discovered that Lucy was a dancer who used her body insistently and to good effect. Almost to my annoyance, I found I was aroused, and clearly she was not unaware of my condition. The tiniest of smiles wafted across her face as she ground against me. After midnight our hostess served a supper of chili. Finally everyone said it was time to turn in, and we all went upstairs. Lucy's and my rooms were on the same floor. On the landing I kissed her good night lightly on the lips, whereupon she stuck her tongue deep into my mouth. Her hand strayed down to my crotch. When she was next able to speak it was to whisper: I won't be long! She wore silk pajamas, preferred the missionary position, and, when I murmured that it would be prudent for me to withdraw, she murmured back, You don't need to, I've put in my diaphragm. She was the first girl I had slept with who was so equipped. That's all that happened. Why was there no sequel, not even the following night, while we were still under the same roof? It's hard to tell, across the wide expanse of time, but I was a mediocre lover, lacking both talent and stamina, a deficiency that didn't prevent me from having brief liaisons, sometimes more than one at a time. But these episodes—really that's all they were—didn't leave a strong impression on me or, I fear, on the objects of my attentions. As one of them, a British photographer, told me disobligingly, I seemed to enjoy the company of women without liking sex. All that changed with the advent of Bella.

Philip, Lucy asked raising her voice, have you fallen asleep? What would you like to drink?

I repeated her question stupidly and answered: Would a gin martini be possible?

Only if you make it, she said, and marched me into the pantry.

I mixed a huge one while she watched. A voice out of the unconscious, where time-defying trivia lie in wait for occasions such as this, prompted me: She'd like a highball, long on the Johnnie Walker Red Label I saw on the pantry counter and short on the soda but with plenty of ice. The same unerring voice predicted the hors d'oeuvres she would serve: cottage cheese with canned minced clams on Ritz crackers, set out on a small round Canton-blue export tray.

Suppose Rip van Winkle had awakened and found that everything was just the same, I said. That's me. Here I am decades later and this place looks exactly the way I remember it. The same admirable furniture, the same dyspeptic ancestors. Most people redecorate at some point, change things around. I like stability. I'm happy to be here.

Goodness, Philip, she said, this must be the first unsolicited compliment you've made me. Will there be more? Actually, keeping this big apartment after that monster decamped and Jamie took off for boarding school is the only good decision about money I have ever made. When I look back on it, it didn't cost all that much to buy and fix up, and I could sell it today for a fortune. But I don't need to; I can still afford the maintenance, even though the trust and everything else my father and now John have managed has just kept dwindling. I couldn't help it about Father, but I should have never let John near my money. Why don't families get it into their heads something so obvious as the fact that genius for making money isn't passed on from the great-great-great-grandfather to some latter-day twerp just because he's in the direct line of descent? I'll never understand it.

We sat down in the library. It had undergone changes, the addition of a huge flat-screen TV and a Barcalounger, the latter an object I would not have expected to find at Lucy's.

You're shocked, she said. It's ugly but comfortable. I spend many lonely evenings on my Barcalounger watching old movies and trying not to get so drunk I can't get myself to bed. Let's face it, Philip. People have dropped me or died. Or they're soft in the head. I don't blame the dead or the living. Who needs an unglamorous boring old woman at their table? Only other unglamorous old women who think they'll be better off if they're friendly. They even invite old bags who live in the country to stay at their apartment. Anything to have company! I'm not friendly. I go to the ballet, New York City and the ABT, the opera, and the philharmonic, but I go alone. I take a taxi to get to Lincoln Center and the bus to go home. I'm not up to fighting for a taxi after the ballet and everything else lets out. Most of the time, I have a bite to eat here before the performance. *Et voilà!* Not like my life in Paris, or what I had once expected.

I nodded.

Well, then make me another drink.

When I returned from the pantry, she continued. You don't understand what it's like. Why should you? You've got your celebrity. Everybody wants a famous author at their table. You used to know so many people that some of them must still be alive. I bet they all want to be nice to you. Are you still writing?

I told her I was—or was trying to.

Then you've got your work. I have nothing. He took it all away.

The martini had relaxed me. Effect of the liquor or the cataracts I'd agreed to have removed at the end of the summer? This old lady saying one unpleasant thing after another, so different from the young woman I had known and liked, seemed very far away; I saw her indistinctly, as though she were behind a wonderfully diaphanous curtain. Besides, was I hearing her right? Could it be that I had misunderstood because I wasn't paying close-enough attention? I raised my eyebrows and shook my head, hoping to clear it.

Philip, you know perfectly well who I'm speaking about, she said sternly. You've never been dumb, so don't play dumb. I mean that bastard Thomas Snow. He got everything he wanted and left me with nothing. Yes, he got everything he wanted. From me. Get that into your head. Sex. I must have told you that over and over. He was a sex maniac with no gift for sex. Perhaps if I had let him do to me all the things he wanted he would have never left. Money. This apartment was exactly the kind of apartment he thought he should have, and he got to live in it as soon as we moved to New York. You know that I paid for it. All the furniture, all the nice things, were mine. Do you think that living in this place, surrounded by my family furniture and portraits, didn't help him at Kidder? Or the parties we gave here for his precious clients and the people from his office? Primitive boors and bores! And the house in Little Compton that's been in my mother's family for generations? He had the use of it on weekends and during his vacations, and all the while those awful relatives of his were making it unlivable. Can you imagine having Mother and Father Snow and all his cousins right across the bay? An ocean wouldn't have been wide enough. And Jamie! It was his idea, he thought we should have a child so I would have something to live for. Very gracious and generous and dumb. Of course, he was scared that otherwise I'd leave! But once we had Jamie, did he lift a finger to help? Too busy first at the business school and then at the office or too busy going over papers he'd brought home or too tired. But never too tired to go out to a dinner party or to fuck! Remember I said in Paris he needed me? Look at me, Philip! He sure did. Only he didn't need a wife. He needed a live-in whore with a big bank account who'd pay his bills and show him how to live in the great world. Where do you suppose he learned all the moves? From the bookkeeper or the garage owner?

Now Lucy, I interrupted. The guy was brilliant. He was even good-looking. He did very well, far better than anyone had the right to expect. Why don't you stop resenting that and instead take credit for having been a formative influence!

I let him get away with murder, she countered gloomily.

The dinner turned out to be a cold affair: roast chicken

and a rice salad she said she had bought at the combination grocery-and-meat-and-fish market where she did most of her shopping, a green salad she'd made herself, cheese, and a lemon tart from Payard. They were all on the kitchen table, along with a bottle of a California red that she asked me to open. We helped ourselves and carried our plates and glasses to the dining room.

I suppose you've been seeing her, said Lucy after we sat down. Don't ask who: of course I mean her, Jane the celebrity! She's probably interviewed you, so at least you have a professional reason to be polite. She seems to entertain on a grand scale. I follow it on Page Six. That's what he always wanted. Café society. Jamie goes to dinner there every time he comes to New York even if he brings the Chicana, and they stayed with them while Thomas was alive. Do you think it's right for her to invite him now that Thomas is dead? I think it's tactless and cruel, rubbing in all her advantages.

She added: I suppose she invites you all the time.

I couldn't help laughing and told her I doubted that Jane even knew I was in the city.

You had better let her know before she goes to the Hamptons for the summer, Lucy continued. That's if you want to be invited. Or interviewed!

She still has her house out there? I asked. As you see, I don't really keep up.

It's his house, Lucy corrected me, she had the good sense not to marry him until he was rich. Yes, she's kept the house and cavorts with my old friends, people he met through me.

People he met in Little Compton too, not only the city and Hamptons crowd!

Perhaps because she could no longer disregard the look of growing distress on my face, she stopped the onslaught abruptly. After a moment of silence, she said, All right, I can tell you want me to shut up. In that case why don't you pour me some wine and put the rest of the chicken and rice on the table.

I did as I was told, and for some minutes we ate and drank in peace. Since she made no move to clear the table after we had finished, I took the plates and platters into the kitchen and came back with the dessert plates, the cheese, and the tart.

That's good, she said. Don't bother about the dishes. The maid comes in the morning.

She didn't take coffee or tea except for breakfast. It made her too nervous. But the coffeemaker worked, and if I wanted coffee there was a can of Medaglia d'Oro in the refrigerator. Making coffee in her kitchen was just about the last thing I wanted. I decided I'd say goodbye right after dessert.

No coffee for me either, I replied. I have a lot of work and have to make this an early evening.

She took that in, pursing her lips and nodding. Well, well, well, she said. You act surprised to hear how bad things were between Thomas and me. I find it difficult to believe that you didn't see what a rotten marriage it was and that you didn't see it coming. Didn't you know that I should have never married him? Never! Would you like to know why? I suppose you don't care. You didn't care back then, and you don't care now. You just found it amusing, in your perverse way. Why not? You had a front-row seat at the undoing of Miss Lucy De Bourgh. Just the kind of story you like. I should have seen through you.

I said all that was perfect nonsense. I liked her; I had been her friend then and still was. To the extent I had had a tangential connection with the events she was talking about—really limited to meeting Thomas when she introduced him to me in Paris—it was ancient history of which I had only a dim recollection. Afterward, in New York, when she and Thomas were still together, our contacts had been superficial. A small number of perfectly pleasant dinners or drinks. That was all!

Well, well, well, she said once again. So you think that's all you know. Would you like to know more? Hear my story to satisfy your professional curiosity? Aren't decadent New England families a subject that interests you? You've made money writing about us.

I nodded and said, Of course.

It's a long story, she replied, but it's not dull, and I have plenty of time on my hands. We can start now.

I glanced at my watch. It was past ten. Did she think she had to nail me down right then and there because otherwise I'd never come back?

I do want to hear any part of your story you want to tell, I said. As your friend, not some sort of ethnographer, but I really mustn't stay late.

Let's leave all this on the table in that case and move into the library, she answered. And I'll have another highball: like the one you made before only stronger.

I went to bed almost immediately after I got home. The highball had turned into three for her and two for me. Perhaps because I was no longer accustomed to drinking after dinner, I slept badly. The next morning I worked for about three hours, getting nowhere. My prose was flat. I had no verve. When I called it quits it was lunchtime. Once again the weather was perfect. I decided against the cheese and salami in my refrigerator and had an egg-salad sandwich instead at a coffee shop on Columbus Avenue. Afterward I went to the park and sat down on a bench on which my face would be in the full sun. Thoughts of Lucy's monologue oppressed me. That beautiful, intelligent, wickedly funny girl, always ready for a new thrill, had made such a hash of it. I shook my head, as if that gesture could free me of the past, and looked around. The park, as I had observed each time I had found myself in it since I returned from France, looked fresh and lovingly cared for, a condition that not so long ago one would not have thought attainable. In its way it was as good as the best French public gardens. On a bench on the other side of the path, at a forty-five-degree angle from me, sat a young Hispanic couple. The girl was attractive, but I was repelled by her companion's short pointed beard. They were deep kissing, either unaware of my presence or indifferent to it.

A great sadness descended on me. Lucy was old; I was old; Thomas and Bella were dead, along with so many others whose presence I had taken for granted. Bodies rotting where they had been interred or already absorbed into the loam, ashes of others scattered here and there. I had buried Bella at the Montparnasse Cemetery in Paris alongside her mother and grandparents. Her father, still alive at ninety-one when she died, joined them three years later. Even if there was room in the plot, of which I wasn't sure, there was no one left whom I could decently ask to see to my being put to rest there as well. I couldn't imagine saddling my cousin Josiah with a transatlantic burial. I would be cremated, a task either the lawyer who had my testament in his safe or someone in his office could see to with little effort. If my cousin Josiah was alive, he would bury my ashes in the garden of the Sharon house I was leaving to him, under the huge rhododendron outside the window of Bella's office. If he died first, perhaps one of his daughters or granddaughters would do it. Fear of death didn't perturb me, and I no longer worried about the mess I would leave behind: manuscripts and files, mementos, and other wretched personal possessions. My papers would go to a university library that had agreed to house them. The rest could be cast to the four winds. Thus far aging, which I had feared, had not been a great trouble. Except for my full share of childhood diseases, colds that lingered longer and longer, and a nasty bronchitis some years ago, I had never been sick. With the aid of an occasional steroid injection into my back, I could still walk to most destinations I wanted to get to, and at a good clip. My memory was unimpaired. Reading glasses had become a necessity, cataracts were a recent development I was about to deal with, and I had lost some acuity of hearing. The irremediable loss was that of ardor. My sporadic couplings with this or that relatively attractive lady after Bella died had been Pavlovian responses to unvarying stimuli: the lady's availability and the facility of the transaction. I brought each of those sour liaisons to a prompt and I hoped dignified end.

As I pursued those thoughts I could see, out of the corner of my eye, that the young lovers were making progress. The man's hand was in the girl's shirt. She had swiveled; her bare legs lay across his lap. Their eyes were closed. I whispered enviously: "Thy willing soul transpires / At every pore with instant fires . . ." As though on a signal, they sprang up and, hand in hand, hurried to a Central Park West exit.

IV

B Y THE TIME she returned from Paris and met
Thomas at her brother John's wedding reception
it had become clear to her, Lucy said the previous
evening after we had moved into the library, that it was all
over between them. The thing was doomed. Of course, she
should have told him so right away, but too much was going
on around her and in her head, and she couldn't face the
argument and the explanations. Besides, she didn't have to.
In two days, on Monday morning, she was returning to Paris;
then, as soon as she closed the apartment and repacked her
suitcases, she would leave for Geneva. During the dinner that
followed the reception, Thomas had begged her to smuggle
him into her room and let him spend the night, but she had
refused. Even if she had wanted him, which was not the case
that evening, she was dead tired and didn't like the idea of
his sneaking around the corridors in the morning. The house
was filled to the rafters; she'd be risking embarrassing gos-

sip and a blowup with her mother. But she did finally agree to meet him the next morning on the dunes. All he wanted was sex, anytime and anyplace. He'd never gotten it into his head that he had to make it so that she had to have him, had to have him the way you must have food and drink. He was an oversexed capon! As usual, he came too fast and tried to make up for it by going on and on. It was no use. She felt distant—distant and detached—from what he was doing to her body and in her body. The odd thing was that he didn't realize it. Probably he liked it better when she was passive and just let him concentrate on himself, which was all he wanted to do anyway.

You weren't invited to the wedding, she continued, there was no reason why you should have been, but if as a novelist you had wanted to get an idea of how those things were supposed to be done that was the one wedding to attend. Edie, the little goose my brother John married, had been an orphan since the age of ten, when her parents and the pilot were all killed going from one of the British Virgins to another in an absurd single-propeller plane, and the cousins who were her guardians were only too happy to have my parents give the wedding at the big house in Bristol. Not that a reception in San Francisco would have made sense. Edie had gone to Miss Porter's and Smith, and all her friends were on the East Coast. It being John the heir, the parents pulled out all the stops. The house, the lawn, the garden, had never looked better. Lester Lanin came himself and made a little speech about still remembering the time he played at my parents' wedding reception, which was one of the first big society functions he had gotten to do. Veuve Clicquot flowed like a river. John Chafee and Claiborne Pell were both there. Given the competition between them, that was a real coup and said a lot about Father's clout. JFK and Jackie canceled at the last minute, but Lee came, and the president sent a cable that Father read after a fanfare. Naturally, all the family and old family friends were in attendance, as well as a big contingent from San Francisco and John's Harvard friends. Your pal Alex van Buren was there with his wife, that awful Priscilla, and the rest of the van Buren clan. All in all, it was a truly memorable party. But wherever I looked, whom did I see? Thomas Snow in the blue blazer I had bought for him to wear in Europe and, if you please, some sort of white trousers. Perhaps even white flannels. Can you imagine the kid they'd all seen pumping gas dressed up like that? He stuck out like a sore thumb. You couldn't miss him.

Good Lord, I thought, what had she expected? Wasn't she old enough, when she met him, to know that he was not from her milieu?

I think you mean to say, I told her, that he didn't fit in. Why was that a surprise or a reason to decide that the "thing" was doomed?

You don't get it at all, she snapped. It's exactly the contrary. He fit in too well. He was ingratiating himself left and right, and they all loved it. They loved him, even my parents and John. As for Thomas, he was in hog heaven. He had understood from the first that he could use me, and he was being proved right. I hated it. I could see that it was a preview of my future if we remained together.

Did you in fact break up? I asked. The other day, as I was thinking about the old times, I recalled, I am pretty sure accurately, running into Thomas in Cambridge during the spring of his first year at business school. He told me you were in Geneva, but he certainly didn't give me the impression that it was all over between you.

No, she replied, as I said, I hadn't told him. I just stayed away and didn't let him come to Geneva. Where he would have gotten the money for the trip is another question. Probably he'd have tried to borrow it from me. I just couldn't deal with him. It was a bad time, a very bad time, for me.

She was sobbing, but when I moved over to her corner of the sofa and patted her shoulder, she brushed away my hand angrily and told me to get her a drink and bring the mixed nuts from the pantry shelf. When I returned with the whiskey and the nuts, I found that she had pulled herself together. I took advantage of the calm to ask the obvious question. So the next thing that happens is that you change your mind and decide to get married?

It wasn't quite that simple, she answered, and put to me a question of her own. Did you ever happen to meet Hubert Brillard, the Swiss journalist? He used to come to Paris regularly. Very Swiss, very patrician, very handsome?

I nodded. I did remember him. He was the super-Aryan I met occasionally, without exchanging more than a casual greeting, at lunches given by my friend Guy Seurat's publishing house. Brillard was invariably the guest of a fashionable novelist with Algérie Française sympathies published by Guy, who claimed that the fellow's talent made one forgive him his political opinions. Someone, perhaps Guy, had told me that Brillard's father had been an important Swiss rightist politician.

He was the star political editor and columnist at the *Journal de Genève,* Lucy said, which at the time was a great paper. I met Hubert in Paris, when I was still working for *Vogue,* at a dinner given by the guy who ran the *Newsweek* bureau and his wife. I was seated next to Hubert. He offered to walk me home, and on the way told me he was married and had two little daughters. You know what I was like. I asked him to come up to the apartment for a nightcap anyway, and the moment we were inside I grabbed him. I knew what I was doing. He made love like a god—no one had ever fucked me like that. Or since. He explained later it had to do with having been on the Swiss Olympic ski team. The training gave him total control over his body. He stayed in Paris for the rest of that week, and every night we made love until dawn. Later, he'd find reasons to come to Paris to see me. I never knew in advance. He'd call late at night and say, *J'arrive.* After six months of that he said he was sorry but we had to stop. One of his daughters was doing badly at school; his wife was acting suspicious; he didn't quite say he was feeling guilty, but that was what I was supposed to understand. I was unbearably sad. It was early fall. In part because of Hubert I hadn't been home during the summer so, for lack of any other plan, I went to Bristol. Your dear friend Alex used to fuck me when I was still at Farmington and on and off afterward when I was at Radcliffe. He'd have me come down to New York, or else he'd drive up to Boston. When I heard from John he was at the business school, I decided to look him up. Anything was better than sitting around in Bristol and having dinner with my parents and John and Edie. Alex was living in a business school dormitory like everyone else, but being Alex he also had a little apartment on Beacon Hill. That's where he'd have me stay. We had a good time, and I was beginning to think that this was perhaps how things should turn out when, out of the blue, he told me he was going to marry Priscilla Baldwin. The bitch with the face of a horse! She'd been a year ahead of me at Farmington. Everybody hated her and made fun of her fat ass. The really funny thing is that Alex and she are still married. Anyway, Alex gave me Thomas as a going-away present. He must have laughed his head off.

She held out her empty glass.

I made her a highball and returned to my corner of the sofa.

Of course Thomas didn't get it, she resumed. He thought Alex was this great guy doing him a big favor. I didn't get it either; I didn't see it was a poisoned offering. All I knew was that I hadn't been left holding the bag and, for a change, someone loved me and couldn't get enough of me. I don't know what he told you about that trip to Italy, but he wouldn't have told you what I'm going to say now. When he was driving he'd have one hand on the steering wheel and the other in my crotch. He'd scare me out of my wits. Sometimes I had to tell him to pull off the road and let him fuck me in the backseat. It was like an obsession. His ignorance of practically everything was astonishing. I'll never forget having to explain to him when we looked at a Bellini crucifixion at the

Uffizi who the two other guys were on the crosses to the left and the right of Jesus. The garage owner and his wife didn't go to church, so he didn't go to Sunday school. I'll give him credit, though: once I had told him something it stuck in his memory, even if he chose to forget that he'd learned it from me. Anyway, when our Italian tour was finished we drove to Paris, and that's where we said goodbye. Although I'd had second thoughts about getting him invited, I'd gone ahead and done it, and we were going to meet at my brother's wedding. He knew I hadn't decided how long I'd stay in the U.S., and I'd told him there was no chance of my getting a job in Cambridge or Boston or anything like it. The only way I'd live with you, I told him, was if we were married, and you're not ready for that. It was a very hot afternoon, and we were crossing the Tuileries after lunch. I was teasing—I had no intention of marrying him—but I thought it would be fun to hear him protest and carry on about how it wasn't so. But he didn't. I think he was relieved. He was scared to death that I'd say I wanted to get married.

Then the unexpected happened. I was still in Paris, supposed to take a boat at the end of the week, when Hubert called, as always in the middle of the night so he'd get me and not the answering machine. He'd once told me he didn't like leaving traces. When I heard his voice I melted. Literally. I wasn't touching myself or anything, but I was all wet down there. In this great baritone voice he said, I want you, you must come to Geneva. His wife was moving to Zurich to be near her parents; the girls were in boarding school; he needed me. He was getting a divorce. Not that any of it mattered. If he'd told me to skip John's wedding, I'd have done it. What am I saying? If he'd told me to go out of the house in my nightgown and exhibit myself on the boulevards, I'd have obeyed. There wasn't an act of self-abasement I wouldn't have performed on his orders. But he was very kind and said instead that since I clearly had to go to Bristol he was coming to Paris. All he asked was that I move to Geneva as soon as possible. The next three days in Paris made me his slave. Do you remember what a lot of noise I made when I came? With him, I howled.

I drove the Mercedes to Geneva with the top down most of the way, singing old camp songs and spirituals, imagining my life with Hubert. He had told me to meet him at the Hôtel des Bergues. It turned out that he'd reserved an apartment there, on the top floor—a bedroom and a slightly larger living room, both with a view of the lake. I wondered how we were going to fit in it, since I understood that he liked to work at home, but it turned out it wasn't for both of us. Just me. Until the divorce proceedings were decided he was going to live at his old place. That was what his lawyer had advised. We settled into a routine. I went for long walks along the lake and in the old city. Some days I drove out to the country, on one or the other side of the lake. Most evenings we had dinner in my living room, sent up by room service. If I was alone, I'd eat in the hotel restaurant. The food was good, especially the Swiss dishes. Hubert had a whole lot of functions and dinners he had to attend, pretty much as a part of his job, and more often than not he didn't ask me to come along. That was all right with me. His friends were polite but without warmth, and I wasn't sure what they thought about Hubert's bringing me along or about my living in Geneva without any visible occupation. Hubert said it was enough that he introduced me as an American journalist. I thought I should have a more substantial explanation, one that I could also give to my parents, and he came up with the silly idea that I was working on a long article that might become a book about Madame de Staël and her years in Coppet. He gave me a biography that I read quickly in order to sound halfway intelligent, and she began to interest me, but I really didn't care. The only thing that counted was the nights—every night—that he spent with me. He made me beg, pretend I was a bitch up on her hind legs and beg for each thing I wanted him to do. I had to name it very precisely. I was in a trance of sexual contentment. We went on like that until right before Christmas, when he told me that he would spend Christmas Eve and Christmas Day in Zurich with his wife and daughters. That's what Brigitte—that was the wife's name—and he had decided was the responsible thing to do. They didn't want the girls to be upset. Then the day after Christmas, he would take them skiing in Zermatt until the end of their school vacation. I yelled at him. I couldn't stop; I just kept yelling until he hit me, and he walked out, without a word, slamming the door. I thought he'd broken my nose. The bleeding was so bad I couldn't stop it, although I tried everything, pinching my nose, putting ice on it. Finally I called the concierge, and he sent the hotel doctor, a nice roly-poly man who came right away, packed my nose with gauze, and gave me some Miltown and Seconal pills. I didn't even have to tell him what had happened. He'd taken one look at me, shaken his head, and said, *Ah, les hommes . . .*

She broke off and said, I'm not sure I can go on. Get me a drink and for Christ's sake have one too. You make me nervous just sitting there like an old maid. Have you joined AA or something?

She drained the whiskey I brought and held out the empty glass. I made another trip to the pantry, returning with the highball and this time a tin of macadamia nuts. This is good, she said. We didn't have much of a dinner. I'll make the rest of this part of the story short. He didn't call the next morning. No apology, no message, no flowers. Just merciless silence. I hadn't a single friend in Geneva, no one I could turn to. Anyway, if there had been such a person, what would I have said, what could they have done? I felt humiliated, and I had never been so utterly alone. I had always been surrounded by people during the holidays; I'd always been a part of some celebration; how could I hide my shame? What would I say when I called home? That one I figured out: I told Father I was in St. Moritz skiing and would call on New Year's Eve if I could get through. Yes, I was having a great time. He didn't think to ask for a number where he could reach me. I particularly didn't want to lose face with the hotel people—they were the ones who counted just then—so I came up with the idea of asking the concierge to book a *couchette* for me on the night train to Paris. That was where I said I was going to spend the fêtes. Actually, I wasn't sure whether I'd really go to Paris and hunker down at the apartment or pretend to be sick and stay in bed until the New

Year. Another scheme came into my head, and I couldn't get rid of it. It was to throw myself down the hotel stairs, which were carpeted, and pretend I had fallen. I'd fake a concussion or something like it. By that time, it was late, and I had been crying, and I was hungry. I had dinner sent up to the room. When the table was cleared, I asked the waiter to leave the wine and my wineglass and bring another bottle of the same wine. I remember it very well. It was a Fendant de Sierre I had ordered to go with the lake fish I had that evening. White wine has always made me sleep, but nothing was happening. I just sat there, drinking and crying. Finally I got undressed, took a hot bath, put on my pajamas, got into bed, and had a Seconal and a Miltown with the rest of the wine. That didn't do the trick, and I was determined to have a good night's sleep, so I took another Seconal. In retrospect, what happened next is clear, though I have no memory of how it happened. I must have sleepwalked because the next morning, around six, the chambermaid found me splayed on the stairs. Luckily, I was unconscious. I had broken my leg, the pain would have been unbearable, and help wouldn't have come no matter how loud I called. The hotel was almost empty on account of the approaching holidays. My loss-of-face problem was halfway solved: I wasn't the lady who had no place to go for Christmas; I was the lady who had drunk too much Fendant. I didn't care. I was in the hospital. When I returned with my big fat cast the roly-poly doctor found nurses to help me. They slept on a foldout cot in the living room. I refused to be in a clinic. At first the physiotherapist came to the hotel. Later the nurse took me there. Father forced Mother to come over to check up. She realized how much I was drinking and yelled and carried on about how if I didn't check into the clinic to be looked after for my leg and dried out I wouldn't be welcome in Bristol. Also how they'd stop my money, which I knew they couldn't do because of the trust. It wasn't the first time. I mean she'd thrown me out of the house once before, when I got in trouble in my last year at Farmington and wasn't allowed to attend graduation. The head was afraid I'd contaminate the other girls! So I told Mother to fuck herself.

Hubert showed up eventually one evening, cool as a cucumber, took a good look, told me I'd been letting myself go, *Tu t'es vraiment laissée aller, ma vieille,* and asked if my keeper—the nurse had tactfully withdrawn into the bedroom—was always there. Wasn't there some way to send her on an errand, get her to stretch her legs, *se dérouiller les jambes?* The idea wasn't hard to get: he thought I was underfucked. A little sex would put me in gear. I had been drinking little glasses of Fendant, and the feeling of revulsion he had at first inspired slowly yielded to an imperious and monstrous need to be used by him, to descend even deeper into humiliation. I called out to Madame Berthe and said that monsieur would stay for dinner. I'd see her in the morning. She said, *Bien, madame,* and was out the door. I was wearing a long silk peignoir; it was easiest at home with the cast. Getting dressed to go to physiotherapy was a production. I was sitting on a small sofa—I guess you could call it a love seat. He didn't try to undress me. Just spread my legs, hiked up the good one so that my foot rested on the seat, opened his fly, and went at me. There is a

Balthus painting of a girl sitting on such a sofa, her legs open. I've never been able to see that painting without being again in that room with him inside me, without melting the way he always knew how to make me melt. That set the pattern. No pretense of love, no talk about his divorce or how we might live together. He'd call just before coming over, so I'd let the nurse go; sometimes—rarely—he stayed to dinner, but really the point was to relieve himself, like when he needed to go to the toilet. No, I didn't want to end it. I'm not sure I would have known how. But I knew I wasn't well and wasn't going to get better. Not my leg; it was doing just fine. The big cast had come off, and I wore a light, supporting version. I mean me; I wasn't well inside. There was one person I had gotten to know a little in Geneva, an American psychiatrist married to a Swiss woman teaching American eighteenth- and nineteenth-century literature at the University of Geneva. I'd met them at a couple of dinner parties. Bill—that was his name—was also teaching at the university on some sort of contract. I think that's why he was allowed to do analysis, although he couldn't prescribe drugs or that sort of thing. But analysis was anyway all he did. He'd impressed me by his brilliance, and it was nice, when we were surrounded by all those Swiss, to be able to speak to him in English. So I called him and said I was in big trouble. He agreed to see me. After we'd met a couple of times he told me I was in no condition to begin an analysis, which in any case would mean commitment to staying in Geneva longer than I intended—based on what I had told him—but he would try to help me at least through the end of the rehabilitation and physical therapy. Bill didn't get me off the booze or the sleeping pills, or make me stop servicing Hubert, but just being able to talk and talk—I think for the first time ever—without having to watch my step saved me.

Hubert got out of my life, without anybody's help, on the Ides of March. I wonder if he'd planned it that way. He pulled out, wiped himself off on my peignoir, which after the first time he had insisted on my wearing, had a double shot of whiskey, and told me this time it's really over, *Ma petite Lucy, cette fois-ci on se quitte pour de bon.* Brigitte had already moved back to Geneva. Why didn't I hit him on the head with the wine bottle when he bent down to kiss my hand? I guess I was too startled or too scared or both.

Soon afterward Bill began to talk to me about going home and where I would begin real treatment. I told him that the way I felt and looked New York scared me. He suggested Boston or Cambridge. His training analyst was practicing in Cambridge. If he has time, he said, he'll be a good fit. I thought about it and began to have a picture in my mind of living in Cambridge or perhaps on Beacon Hill that filled me with nostalgia and a longing for a place I knew but where nobody would be at me, where there were no complications, where I didn't have to deal with the Swiss or the French. It's funny: of course I knew that Thomas was at the business school, I kept on getting his letters, but I didn't connect the dots and realize that he was one person who'd surely be at me. Not that it would have made any difference. Dr. Reiner could take me. Someone at the trust company found an apartment for me on Louisburg Square, the back of the ground floor with its own entrance and the use of the garden, and I moved in May. Dr. Reiner's advice was devastating, but I was so beaten down I couldn't argue: You need to be in McLean. When you've been dried out and are less hysterical I'll work with you. So that's what I did.

Once again, she was crying. Who was I to blame her or tell her to stop? I tiptoed out of the library, got her another highball, and made one only slightly weaker for myself.

Here, I said, you and I both need them.

She had stopped crying and said, I've got to pee. Back in a minute. There is a toilet you can use off the foyer.

After she returned we drank for a few minutes in silence. Then she said, Even this part of the story is longer than I had thought. I'll finish it in a few words. I was able to discharge myself from McLean toward the end of August, just before Dr. Reiner returned from the Cape. We started treatment, and I made my daily trek to his office in a house at the corner of Sparks and Highland in Cambridge, which was where he also lived. There is sometimes a period at the beginning of treatment, if you hit it off with the analyst, when you surprise yourself by feeling good. That happened to me. A woman I had met when I was still at Radcliffe was a powerful editor at Houghton Mifflin, who later published *The Painted Bird*. She'd been very nice to me and said I should let her know if I ever wanted a job in publishing. I found the courage to get in touch with her; she remembered me and put me to work, at first reading manuscripts and later line editing. It turned out

I could do that well; there's never been anything the matter with my English. All of us in the family speak well and can write clear prose—even Mother and my brother John. The only trouble with them is that they've got nothing to say.

And now I'm really tired, she said. You'd better go home.

V

A HANDWRITTEN NOTE thanking Lucy for dinner and saying I had been profoundly moved by all she had told me about Geneva seemed nicer and more friendly than an e-mail. Next morning I walked briskly in the park, a regime I was trying to impose on myself, took a bath, and wrote to Lucy. Her apartment building was near enough to the NY Society Library, where I intended to spend the afternoon doing research, for me to decide to go there on foot and deliver the letter personally, instead of putting it in the mail. However, after the doorman had examined the envelope he announced that Mrs. Snow had left for the country. He'd forward my letter with the rest of her mail. Her not having mentioned the imminent departure struck me as odd, but the reprieve was welcome. I wouldn't need to see her again any time soon. That evening I sent her an e-mail saying that a proper letter was on its way and wishing her a good summer. She answered immediately, explaining that she had rushed off to Little Compton to attend an emergency town meeting about a proposal to widen a road near her property and would be back after the weekend. The doorman was an idiot: he should be holding her mail instead of forwarding it. She would call in the morning to straighten him out. Would I be in New York when she returned? Could we have dinner? She wasn't moving to the country for the summer until the Fourth of July weekend. I answered that I'd be around and would look forward to seeing her.

As it happened, I was planning to be away during the weekend as well, at my place in Sharon. The real estate agent had assured me that the tenant to whom I'd been renting the house during the academic year—Peter Drummond, a political science professor at Bard—and his partner, a composer whom I'd met several times without managing to remember his name, had left it in apple-pie order, just as in the past years. Nonetheless, it seemed best to see for myself and perhaps arrange for a fresh coat of paint in the kitchen, living room, and my bedroom. It had occurred to me as well that since I had given up my apartment in Paris and would be living in New York it might be nice to be able to use the Sharon house year-round. Before making a final decision, I wanted to find out from the agent how much it would cost to keep the house heated through the winter and to have my long and twisting driveway plowed. I was also concerned about Peter and whether he would find it difficult to relocate. If that were the case, I'd give him at least a year's notice. I was going to leave on Friday morning, which gave me a couple of days when I could see Thomas Snow's widow, Jane, a project

I'd had in mind ever since I'd arrived in the city. Lucy's rants had somehow imbued it with new interest. Jane had remarried, but I had not met her husband and had in fact forgotten his name as well. All the same, finding her couldn't be a problem. The weekly show of her interviews with authors, on which I had twice appeared, continued to be aired on public television. I had no doubt that my editor's assistant had her office telephone number or would know how to get it.

Lucy's sneer about Jamie's visits to his stepmother, however, led me to think that most probably she was still living in Thomas's Park Avenue apartment, the location of which, south of Seventy-Second Street and on the desirable west side of the avenue, I now realized, must be one more thorn in Lucy's side. Accordingly, the next morning, before turning to the young man at the publishing house or Google, I dialed Thomas's old number and asked to speak to Jane Morgan. As I might have expected, given the anemic sales of my two most recent books, my name clearly meant nothing to the secretary who answered and proceeded to grill me at annoying length. In the end I passed the test, and Jane came to the telephone. She sounded enthusiastic about getting together and introducing me to her husband Ned and wondered aloud which would be better: the three of us having dinner, or she and I first having lunch à deux and going over the old times. I expressed a slight preference for the latter solution. My familiar haunts on the Upper East Side had all apparently disappeared or were no longer establishments where someone like Jane would wish to be seen, but she suggested a French restaurant on Lexington Avenue not far from her apartment. We could meet there at one, this being a day when she didn't have to be at the studio. She said she'd make sure we had a quiet table.

She was still a knockout and didn't look a day older than the last time I'd seen her—not surprising in one who had surely always watched her figure and her complexion but somehow very comforting and pleasant. I was discovering that seeing people my own age or, as in Lucy's case, only four or five years younger gave me little pleasure. It was all very well to recall a shared past, but what I really wanted was a bridge to the present. We devoted the unavoidable ten minutes to the folly of the Iraq adventure and another five minutes to John Kerry and his promising but oddly lethargic candidacy. Ned is working for his campaign, she told me. He'll be interested in talking to you about how you and other writers can help. In turn I told her that I knew some of the senator's Forbes cousins, had been thinking along the same lines, and had been frustrated by the difficulty of volunteering to do anything other than send money.

Ned will open the door, she replied. You'll have to come to dinner very soon. Even better, spend a weekend with us in Water Mill.

After a pause, she asked how I had been passing my time now that I was back in New York.

First of all working, I said. I'm close to completing the first draft of a book.

A novel? she asked.

I nodded, whereupon she told me she had, of course, read my latest and how sorry she had been that scheduling problems had prevented her from attempting to prevail on me to find the time for an interview.

That sort of hypocrisy being both familiar and odious, I was at the point of erupting but managed to restrain myself. There was no point in spoiling this lunch and perhaps queering the chances of her taking up the new novel. So I smiled and went on with the account of my activities.

I've been putting my apartment in order, I said. Two young relatives, my cousin Josiah Weld's granddaughters, had been living there for almost three years. My old housekeeper kept an eye on them, but all the same the kids left traces that had to be removed. I stayed at the Harvard Club while that was done and the stuff that had gone to storage was brought back. Other than that? I haven't particularly wanted company, which is just as well, since so few of the people I used to see in New York are still living in the city or indeed are alive and operational. I've gone to the movies and once to the ballet. That's how I ran into Lucy, I added, at the ballet. Then, a couple of days ago, she had me to dinner at her apartment—alone!

You lucky man, Jane remarked speaking very slowly, that must have been fun, and very enlightening—about Thomas and me! I'm glad you've decided to give me equal time.

Actually, I replied, you got off fairly easily, although she does wish her friends hadn't abandoned her for you. She did have a good deal to say about poor Thomas.

What an awful woman! Jane fired back. When you think how she terrorized him! Thomas, who dominated every meeting he went to, who mesmerized heads of great corporations, central bankers, politicians, cabinet ministers, would just want to hide, crawl under the nearest piece of furniture, when she telephoned, and since most of the time it was about Jamie there was no way he could refuse to take the call. You know how her voice carries. I couldn't help overhearing unless I left the room, and he'd make these desperate signs for me to stay. Now Thomas, she'd say, don't you understand this and that. Now Thomas, don't play dumb, you know I'm right, Jamie really needs this or that. No, there is no other way. Or, Do you realize how you are destabilizing him? She'd use this snarky psychobabble on him, as if she'd studied at Freud's knee instead of wasting untold years and money on the couch of a preposterous Central Park West shrink. Dr. Peters thinks this, Dr. Peters says that, now Thomas, Dr. Peters is concerned about Jamie's autonomy! It used to make me sick to hear it.

She did say that Jamie is a failure. It's really too bad; I remember him as such a nice little boy and then a nice and attractive teenager.

Don't let her bad-mouthing turn you against him either. He is still a truly nice man, sweet and gentle, and he's a failure only if you think every screenwriter is a failure if he doesn't get an Oscar or write the equivalent of *The Sopranos*! He's done well at Sundance and in Toronto, and he has something right now in Cannes. He's making a living, and he likes what he's doing. Sure, Thomas helped him, and the money he left him has taken the pressure off. What's wrong with that? What is a father supposed to do with his money? The truth is that he liked what Jamie wrote and understood how stupid it would have been to say, Listen, kid, you should write better or be more commercial, or If you can't write better and earn more money then at least learn to count and I'll take you into the firm! Thomas and Jamie had a really good relationship. Jamie trusted him. Some of that has rubbed off on me. He trusts me too. And you know what? I wish he were my son.

We had ordered our lunch. Jane's choices amused me: a mixed-green salad followed by a Caesar salad, both without dressing, and a Perrier. So that's what going out to lunch was about. Small wonder that the owner of my own favorite French restaurant, the last of the breed that could trace its ancestry to the 1939 World's Fair, had trouble hanging on to his middle-aged clientele, never mind acquiring a young one. I wasn't going to play Simon Says. So I asked for *pâté de campagne* followed by a hanger steak—rare—and a glass of Côtes du Rhône. I guess she had found my order amusing too and remarked that I hadn't lost my Parisian habits. That too would be right up Ned's alley.

I bet she gave you the Thomas-the-monster routine, she continued, especially if you haven't seen her since he died. Don't let her. You knew him too well to buy that sort of crap.

Jane was wrong there. I had genuinely liked Thomas and had had a good opinion of him, but I also knew that wife beaters and child molesters often come across as nice guys. It all depends on the frequency of your contacts and the angle of vision. But my curiosity, mixed with regret, had been aroused, and I intended to learn more.

Yes, I did hear that he was a monster, I told her, and doubtless it's not the last time if I see her again, which I think I will.

But Lucy mostly talked about herself. I think the point was to explain why she married Thomas in the first place—when she knew all along it was a mistake. The monster part had to do with his having used her money and, I guess, social position to climb and never giving anything back. And of course, anyway at the start, with his having been so wrapped up in his work that he left her to cope with Jamie alone and so forth. But principally it was about having been used.

I was going to continue, although naturally without mentioning the complaints about sex, but Jane raised her hand to stop me. Look, she said, Thomas put up with a lot of craziness, and I mean real craziness. By all means, listen to her and reach your own conclusions and, if you don't mind, share them with me if ever the time comes. I'll give you my own take. For now, just two things. First, he wasn't a closet Frankenstein monster. Second, don't go for lies and fabrications about how Thomas and I got together. I didn't have an affair with him before he and Lucy split. Thomas and I knew each other socially because Horace Jones, my first husband, was—and he still is—a partner in a law firm that worked on a lot of Kidder's M-and-A deals, including Thomas's deals, when Thomas was still at Kidder. Afterward, when Thomas and Tim Carroll started the new firm, they kept on giving work to Horace. But there was nothing between Thomas and me. Zero. And it's a lie that I left Horace because I had my eye on Thomas. I left him because he'd had one office romance too many. Perhaps you wonder why the law firm didn't boot him out on account of the office hanky-panky which, by the way, according to my moles over there, continued? That was, in principle, what the firm did at the time. The reasons are that at first they didn't want to lose the Kidder business, which they thought, because he did so much work for Thomas, depended on his staying at the law firm and, later, after Thomas left Kidder and founded his own firm together with Tim Carroll, because they didn't want to lose the Snow Carroll business. That's right, Snow Carroll business. Thomas and Tim talked it over when Thomas and I started going out, and they decided to keep using Horace. Thomas was very clear about it. I've got Jane; Horace has lost her; he does a good job; why should I want to punish him? So don't forget to say hi to Lucy!

Saying hi to Lucy had to wait. I packed some clothes and the indispensable minimum of books, took the train to Wassaic, where my car was in storage, and, my sense of anticipation and disquiet mounting, drove over the Connecticut line to Sharon. The house looked good, and so did the garden. During a quick tour of the property, I checked as always first the trees and flowering bushes that I considered Bella's, planted by her or at her instigation. They had survived well the winter storms that had hit the valley. So had the peonies, Bella's favorites; for the first time since she died, I wasn't missing the moment of their greatest glory. Inside, the house was cold and naked, Peter Drummond and the composer had removed their photographs and knickknacks, and my personal possessions were still in the locked guest-room closets, but otherwise it was fine. On the kitchen table I found a note from the real estate agent, asking me to call. I'll come right over, he said when I reached him. It turned out that he had news from Peter. Renting from me had worked out well, and he and Ezra Morris—he reminded me that that was the composer's name—had gotten to like Sharon and the surrounding area so much they'd been looking for an affordable house to buy. Recently, the Browns' place had come on the market, Sally Brown the widow having died of a stroke in December. The contract with the estate had been signed, and they expected to take possession in mid-June. So in the end it was Peter giving me notice rather than the other way around. The agent said I shouldn't worry about being stuck without a tenant for the winter; he was sure he could find a replacement, perhaps another academic. I told him the truth: I felt relieved. Since I was going to live in New York, it seemed right to be able to use the house all year, the way Bella and I had done, and now I could carry out my plan without guilt feelings about taking it away from those nice people.

The other side of the coin, which I obviously didn't mention to the agent, was the incipient panic into which the news of Peter and Ezra's departure and the consequent reality of what I intended to do had thrown me. The heating bills, and plowing out my driveway weren't the real problem; I had decided not to bother about them. The totality of the undertaking unnerved me. It was one thing to think idly about how nice it would be to leave the city and go to Sharon on crisp fall and winter weekends, perhaps even over Christmas and New Year's, and another to face the implications: seeing to the cleanup and planting in the spring, worrying about the marauding deer, putting up netting to keep them off the flower beds, deadheading and weeding, the fall cleanup and putting the garden to sleep for the winter—I had let it all go since Bella died, having immediately asked the real estate agent to find a responsible tenant who'd relieve me of all those tasks. It wasn't the need to do the work that troubled me: I was capable of doing some of it, although Bella's fondness for gardening had led her to take most of it off my hands. And I knew perfectly well that the landscaping firm that mowed the lawn and the two meadows and had always done the spring and fall cleanup and planted trees and the larger bushes for us would happily take full charge of the grounds. Just as between Mrs. James, my veritable pearl of a housekeeper, and Bob the handyman, all my other creature comforts would be seen to very nicely. The house would be spick-and-span, and its grounds carefully tended, my laundry done, and my clothes cleaned and mended. In fact Mrs. James, aided by Doris, her elementary-school-teacher daughter, would probably like nothing better than to do the shopping and cook my guests' and my food. It was a cinch, provided *tutti quanti* received checks on time and in the appropriate amounts. Yes, those very good people, whom I'd known and trusted over so many years, who had loved Bella and been so kind during her terrible last year, were still my friends. They'd make sure I received the finest care in my hospice built for one. The checks weren't a problem. Unless I lived far too long, my savings would be sufficient, and if they were exhausted, the Sharon, Connecticut, hospice would close its doors, and Medicaid, if it still existed, would have one more old geezer busting a hole in its budget. No, it wasn't a question of money; it was the utter futility of my existence, the books I was writing included. I realized that I was trembling and said to myself, Stop it, Bella would be ashamed of you. You've managed all right here in the summers. If using the house the rest of the year doesn't work out, you'll put it on the market and get your fresh air in Central Park.

Feeling calmer, I had a cup of tea, called the handyman and asked him to stop by the next morning to talk about painting and minor repairs, made a list of staples to pick up at the supermarket, and puttered around trying to make the house look and feel less unlived in. Then I sat down at my worktable and during a few hours actually managed to write. It grew dark, and for once it was hunger and the desire for a drink, rather than the flow of words turning into a trickle, that made me stop. I saved and backed up the new text and put my laptop to sleep. There were a couple of bottles of gin in the liquor closet. I made myself a gin and tonic, ate a handful of Ritz crackers out of a box left behind by Drummond & Co., and tried my cousin Josiah's Kent, Connecticut, number. I was in luck. He and his wife were in residence and were free the next evening. I deflected the invitation to have dinner at their house and asked them to come instead to Sharon and help me start a new chapter of my tattered existence. As an afterthought I added the injunction to bring any child or grandchild who showed up in the meantime. Buoyed momentarily by a vague sense of accomplishment, I set out for a pizza at a roadhouse outside Sharon.

. . .

Josiah and Molly did bring their granddaughters Natasha and Nina, the two squatters who had occupied my apartment, and Natasha's boyfriend, a baby-faced fellow with a wispy blond beard and a stud in his right earlobe. I was convinced that the choice of a stud over an earring, as well as its placement, had coded meanings, but didn't dare to inquire. Instead I asked Zeke whether he was, like the girls, a recent college graduate and was both surprised and amused to hear that he had a graduate degree in computer science from MIT and was working on valuation models for, of all places, Snow Carroll. I told him that I had first met Thomas Snow just before he went to business school and had kept in touch with him until the end. Zeke replied that I had been really lucky. Obviously, in his mind my friend Thomas was a great man. My amusement deepened when Nina told me that she too worked at Snow Carroll, but on mergers and acquisitions, and that it had been she who introduced Zeke to Natasha.

Mrs. James announced that dinner was served. Not knowing how many we would be, I had bought a large leg of lamb at the supermarket, with the idea that it would either be eaten by an indeterminate number of Welds or see me through several lunches and dinners to come, and was relieved that it had come out of the oven just the way Bella would have cooked it. Mrs. James had taken care of the potatoes, green beans, and salad, and I had picked up, also at the supermarket, an apple tart. My memory had turned out to be correct: there were cases of wine in the cellar left over from the time when I'd buy wine young and let it mature undisturbed. Some of it was ready. I sat across from Josiah, having put Molly at the head of the table, and after I had uncorked the third bottle and given it to Zeke to pour, I told Josiah that I had run into Lucy at the ballet and had subsequently had dinner at her house and had also lunched with Thomas's widow.

Quite a coincidence, he replied, Thomas and his firm seem to be all around us!

It turned out that he had done a number of deals with Thomas, both while Thomas was still at Kidder and afterward. Molly and he had also seen Thomas and Jane as a couple socially with some frequency. That had not been the case when Lucy was still around. Molly didn't take to her; she'd disliked the way Lucy talked on and on, determined to dominate every conversation, and the disagreeable tension between her and Thomas.

And what was your opinion of him? I asked.

As a financier—that's simple, I admired him. At Kidder he was one of the best they had. Some people said he was the best of our age group in the city—which really means the country—and I believe that. His and Tim Carroll's timing when they left their nice secure partnerships and started their firm—a very gutsy decision, let me tell you—was perfect, and I happen to know it was Thomas who really called the shots. I don't need to tell you that the firm has been a brilliant success in a rough business and in rough markets. Retiring when he did was gutsy too. He was plenty rich, but he must have realized that the really big money was still to come. But he wasn't greedy; there was more than enough for Jane and Jamie and his foundation, and he wanted to write and teach at least part-time and do all the other things he could suddenly do without a conflict with the firm or having people attack the sincerity of his views by pointing to the firm's business. I'll give you an example. Under his leadership the firm took some huge and very successful speculative positions, selling currencies or commodities short or building up long positions. And he'd been up to his ears in solving sovereign-debt problems. People who disagreed with this or that article or op-ed piece he wrote for the FT could and did say that what the firm had done was inconsistent with what he was preaching. So he was one hundred percent right to cash out. As a person? In some ways he came across as standoffish, perhaps cold. No small talk. Fundamentally a square. That's what was said about him. It wasn't my experience. He was always very nice in his dealings with me both in business and socially. I had the impression, anyway in the beginning, that my being your cousin counted in the equation. As a friend? Very reliable. He wrote letters of recommendation to every school the kids have ever applied to, and let me tell you they were good letters. All the same, I think he had very few friends aside from those he made at business school or perhaps before. The rap about being a square? It was deserved. He read nonfiction—biography, history. Probably he hadn't read a novel since A *Tale of Two Cities* in high school. Ballet? He didn't go, and he didn't much like the opera either. He told me about his background. I always thought that deep down he remained a boy from a small town who'd made good. Of course—Josiah laughed—Newport's a very special small town!

He paused and held out his glass, which I filled, Zeke having put the bottle in my proximity, and, seemingly changing the subject, asked: Are you a member of the Paddock?

I shook my head and said, No, no one has ever suggested it.

How did you escape it? Somebody must have screwed up. I am, Josiah continued, and so is Alex van Buren. You surely remember him? Probably he qualifies as Thomas's oldest friend. Come to think of it, I am almost sure it was he who put up Thomas for the club. Anyway, he has lunch there practically every day. If you're trying to reconstruct an image of Thomas, Alex is the man to talk to. The stuff he remembers is amazing. Give me a call when you get back to the city. I'll take you to lunch and you can have a go at Alex.

Alex! I said. Holy cow! This is turning into paleontology, but you've got a deal. I'll be in touch next week.

Josiah was my favorite cousin. I was his best man when he married Molly. He and she were one of the few married couples of my generation who had never split, never divorced, and were, insofar as one could tell, still in love with each other, still genuinely happy. As happy, I hoped, as I had been with Bella. I followed them out to their car and, as we said goodbye, told them how grateful I was for their visit.

Next time in Kent, said Molly. Then it was the girls' turn. We embraced, and Natasha said, Uncle Philip, we want you to know that we still really miss Aunt Bella.

I covered my face with my hands. Tears were running down my cheek.

VI

WHEN I GOT BACK to the city I found a message from Lucy on my answering machine. She complained at length that Little Compton had been dreary, she'd seen no one except her awful cousin Harry Goddard and his second wife who disliked her, the cocktail party she'd gone to had been a disaster, and the road was approved the evening before she arrived, meaning that her visit was a total waste. She concluded by inviting me to dinner at her apartment anytime during the week. We'll have cold chicken, like the last time, she said, or if you're tired of cold chicken—I never tire of it myself—I'll get a steak and you can cook it.

I didn't want to let myself in for a talk therapy session as long as the last one. The obvious trap being those after-dinner drinks, I called her back and invited her instead to the restaurant where I had lunched with Jane. She had told me I could use her name when I made a reservation and that if I did I would get a quiet table and be treated with the respect due a great novelist. That is how she had introduced me to the owner or manager, a trim and suave man called Gérard. I had hesitated for a moment before naming the restaurant, reflecting that it would be amusing, but also potentially embarrassing, to find that Jane and her husband were at the next table. Then I remembered her saying that this bistro was her favorite at lunch, but she never used it in the evening. Far from objecting to my choice, Lucy said, My my, you stay away from the city for years, and in no time at all you get to rejoin the smart set.

My date with her was for Thursday. I had no other engagements during the week and decided that since my book seemed to be moving forward I could afford the time it would take to have lunch with Josiah and, if he turned up, Alex van Buren. Josiah was free. We agreed to meet at the Paddock on Wednesday at one.

The custom of the club was for members, even if accompanied by guests, to have lunch in the members' dining room, at a long glistening mahogany table. It was possible for the member and his guest to have lunch at a small individual table in the adjoining dining room, but if we did, Josiah pointed out, we'd miss Alex, who never set foot there. After we'd had our glass of champagne at the bar—Josiah's lunchtime drink, which he took in a large brandy snifter over one ice cube—and made our way to the dining room, we found that there were several men clustered at the near end of the table. Josiah greeted them with a nod and a wave of the hand and led me firmly by the elbow to the far end. Let's sit on this side, he said, where we can talk without getting involved in the general chitchat. I'll watch out for Alex. In the meantime, let's order. I'm starved.

I knew him instantly. Josiah having half risen from his chair, he headed in our direction without it being clear whether he had recognized me. Alex had always been a big man, but now he had become huge, as large as his father, whom I remembered as a sort of giant. The light gray pinstriped suit he wore was of such exquisitely old-fashioned cut that I was ready to bet it had been his father's. Probably it hadn't even been necessary to cut it down. He had aged, but he was still a beautiful man, his face a healthy pink, the blue eyes clear and unencumbered by glasses, the cheeks firm, and the brow smooth. He was someone, it would have been easy to think, who had never known a moment of worry.

Philip, he said weightily after he'd sat down and told the waiter over his shoulder he'd have the usual, Philip, we don't see you here much. That is really too bad. Members prominent in the arts should lunch and dine at the club often and bring in talented youngsters of the right sort. Not too many, of course, not too many. That was my motto at the *Lampoon* too. We needed you super gifted fellows but not in numbers that might make the rest of us uncomfortable. Remember your competition? I remember it as though it were yesterday!

Of course I do, I replied. If you hadn't helped I wouldn't have gotten in.

That was the truth. Candidates for membership in the humor magazine, known as Phools, were required to perform a prank in Harvard Square that was evaluated for the requisite "Phoolishness" by upperclassman members. It was the last trial before the members' vote. I was a freshman, and I could think of nothing better than to appear on Massachusetts Avenue on April 1, in blazing sunshine, with the temperature in the sixties, dressed up as Santa Claus, ringing my bell and trying to collect change from anyone entering Hayes-Bickford's, the hangout we all went to for English muffins and tea. My stunt was judged "derivative and jejune" by all except Alex, who argued for my election, proclaiming that my stunt proved I was going to be the magazine's Tristan Tzara. His voice carried the day, and I suppose I had been insufficiently grateful ever since.

You've proved me right. You're one of our brightest ornaments. But I must say that while you were on the magazine you were singularly unfunny!

Alex laughed so hard at his own display of wit that he began to cough and choke, turning so red in the face that an alarmed waiter took it upon himself to hit him between the shoulder blades.

Harder, he gasped, harder.

The choking fit at last under control, he returned to the subject of my not making sufficient use of the club.

I believe you spend a good deal of the time in Paris, he told me, but that's not a reason for not doing your duty as a good citizen and lunching here when you're in town. Unless men are willing to do their bit—

Hold on, Alex, interrupted Josiah, for some reason Philip isn't a member!

A ridiculous oversight, replied Alex, one that can and will be corrected. By the way, do you remember poor Thomas Snow? I put him up for membership here even before he made partner at Kidder. It wasn't a joyride, I can tell you. Just as you'd expect, some fellows on the admissions committee raised questions about his background, not having been in any club at college, and so forth. I managed to beat them back. It helped that my old man had been crazy about Thomas from the time he tutored the kiddies in Newport and that I could report how Al Gordon had told the old man he thought the world of young Snow. Father and Al were thick as thieves. Our firm cleared through Kidder. You want to hear something that really made me laugh? You both know Lucy—Lucy De Bourgh, who was married to Thomas? Believe it or not, after Thomas told her he'd been asked to join the Paddock and that it was my doing, she called me at the office to give me a piece of her mind. Fit to be tied! The idea was that Thomas had already gotten too big for his britches, and I had no business aiding and abetting his self-aggrandizement! I swear to God that's what she said. I laughed and laughed. Well, getting you in will be a breeze. No problems with your background. Unless someone objects there's too much sex in your books.

Alex began to laugh again, irrepressibly. Fortunately, the waiter had been hovering behind his chair and administered three preventive whacks that made Alex able to finish his black bean soup.

That is hardly believable, I said. By the way, it so happens I've run into Lucy; in fact I had dinner with her two weeks ago. Seeing her made me think about the old times, and I remembered Thomas Snow telling me back then that he met her through you, of all people!

Yes, I'll take the credit for that, Alex replied. In fact I deserve more credit for various good deeds than you probably realize. If you and she talked about the old times, you must have gotten a blast about me.

Actually, I didn't. Most of the grousing was about Thomas. But she's asked to see me again, and I wouldn't be surprised if I heard more.

Alex raised his eyebrows and said, You may be playing with fire. Am I right, didn't your very beautiful French wife die some time ago?

I nodded.

Well, you must forgive me. My memory is still pretty good about the past, especially if at the time I focused on the events, but sometimes it plays games. For instance right now I can't remember whether Priscilla or I wrote to you when it happened. The fact is—I don't need to tell you—that everybody's been dying left and right. I've given up reading the *Times* obits, though Priscilla still does. One could spend all one's time writing letters of condolence. So you're a widower! Quite a catch for the likes of Lucy. And she hasn't talked to you yet about how she and Thomas split?

I shook my head.

You're having dinner with her? That's probably somewhere on the menu. Check with me before you swallow what she serves up! And write down your address for me. I'm going to send you the club's yearbook so you can look through the membership roster and pick out names of people in the club you know whom I can ask for letters of support. You remember my one-and-only wife, Priscilla, don't you? You used to dance with her in the days of our ill-spent youth. How silly! Of course, you do! She'll be delighted to hear you've resurfaced. Speaking of Lucy, there's no love lost between those two. The feelings go all the way back to when they were at Miss Porter's. You and Priscilla will have a great talk, comparing notes. These days we let the ladies into the guests' dining room on Thursday evenings. We'll have dinner here. And turning to Josiah, he added, You and Molly had better join us. Priscilla always takes charge. She'll work it out.

Feeling certain that I would hear more about Lucy without waiting for the dinner with Priscilla, I was all agog, but at that precise moment three wondrously thin clubman types, highball glasses of what looked like bullshots in hand, wandered into the room and scanned the table looking for a place to perch. Having spotted Alex, they made a beeline for him. Two sat down flanking him, the third next to Josiah. Introductions followed. Perfect timing, perfect timing, intoned Alex and, addressing the clubman on his right, said, Can you imagine anything so scandalous, Junius? Young Philip here, a distinguished novelist and my *Lampoon* protégé, isn't a member! I intend to set that right. Turning to me, he explained: Junius is our president.

Josiah and I had been served our coffee, and shortly afterward we rose from the table.

Remember, don't let her brainwash you, Alex called out. And mum's the word. He put his finger to his lips.

. . .

Not long after I married Bella, needing income during a dry spell between two books, I did a series of articles on cultural subjects for *LIFE,* which then paid remarkably well, including profiles based on extensive interviews with Vladimir Horowitz, Pablo Casals, Yehudi Menuhin, Eugene Ionesco, and Kingsley Amis. Ultimately, these pieces became a book that paid for rewiring of the Sharon house, putting on a new roof that didn't leak, and installing modern amenities such as central heating, a hot water boiler, and an efficient pump. Bella joked that we lived in a house that *Rhinoceros* built. I might have continued to do journalism if *LIFE* hadn't changed or the plot of a new novel that went on to win important prizes hadn't taken shape in my mind. My dormant interviewer's instincts, developed and honed during that period, had become aroused. As I was walking across the park the next day to meet Lucy, I pretty much decided to try the shock-question technique and ask straight out whether, in spite of her long-standing dissatisfaction, it was true that, as she had hinted, it was actually Thomas who chose to leave. In that case, what had precipitated the crisis? As I waited in the restaurant, however, I began to have doubts. Certainly she was lonely and had a seemingly overpowering desire or need to justify herself and perhaps also to take revenge on the dead man. But unlike a celebrity who might play hard to get but has her eye on the end product, the big spread with flattering photos in a glossy magazine, Lucy couldn't look forward to any reward for putting up with me. It would be stupid to spook her. There was also something to be said for letting her talk at her pace and in her own way. She might say more than she had intended if I didn't interfere with her stream of consciousness.

She arrived fifteen minutes late. I told her quite sincerely that I hadn't minded. It was pleasant to sip a martini and eavesdrop on conversations at other tables. The way I lived now, I could go for days hearing no human speech other than that on the radio or when the doorman says, Have a nice day, sir.

And how do you think I live? she countered.

The hint of unprovoked aggression in that remark made me look at her more carefully. She was haggard, and I could see reddish blotches on her face, imperfectly covered by makeup. It could be an allergy to something in her garden; she had returned from the country only two days before. I offered her a glass of champagne, which she refused, and she asked for a martini like mine. There was a leak in her swimming pool, she told me, that couldn't be fixed without emptying it and pouring some cement; in all probability she'd need a new heater; the pool man was a crook. She wouldn't trust him with the repairs and wished she hadn't quarreled with his predecessor, who was also dishonest but on a smaller scale and at least knew what he was doing. She'd called the trust company to say she'd need money for the repairs and the heater, and the trust officer's assistant had been rude to her. When she complained to her brother John, he told her that the De Bourgh trusts were no longer among the trust company's very important clients. He had the gall to tell her that it was her fault if the people at the trust company weren't nice to her. She had alienated—"alienated" was the word he'd actually used—everyone there by being a constant pain in the ass. Of course, she hung up on him, but that didn't solve the problem. There was no way she could fire the trust company. It was written into the trust. And obviously no one was going to help her bring them to heel! That's what her Friday had been like. On Saturday, there was a party at the McGregors', the next house over. At least they had the decency to invite her. She couldn't imagine why they had invited about half of the other guests. Her great-aunt Helen Goddard King, who had left her the Little Compton house in her will, wouldn't have let them in the door. She couldn't believe that any of them had gotten into the club, not even as summer members. Not that she cared. She hardly set foot in there anymore.

I interrupted and got her to tell the waiter what she wanted for dinner and ordered my own meal and a bottle of wine. It didn't seem impossible, unless I put her on another track, that this particular jeremiad would stop only after I'd paid the check and told her I'd walk her home.

Look, I said, I've been thinking a great deal about those terrible months in Geneva and the remarkable new start you made in Cambridge, and there is something I obviously haven't gotten right. I think you told me that before you went to Geneva you had decided that you and Thomas were through, that it wasn't going to work. Indeed, you joined Hubert without any thought for Thomas. And then you and Thomas get married anyway! Why? The other question that has been rattling in my head is why you didn't continue your career in publishing. It seems like such a perfect fit.

The second question is easy, she replied. I liked Emily Calhoun, my boss at Houghton Mifflin; I liked the publishing house in Boston. I liked the nice fuddy-duddy men who worked there. They'd all gone to St. Mark's and served in the navy, and it was nice to go with them to the Ritz for lunch in the café. They liked martinis, and so did I, and I knew they would have given their left testicle to take me upstairs and get me undressed. I'm not sure they even wanted more than that, but whatever it was they wanted, they never dared to make a move. In New York, I was too sick, and I had Jamie. When he started kindergarten I had a couple of interviews. It wasn't for me, even if I had felt better and Thomas hadn't made me feel completely worthless. Those men in New York publishing houses, those second-raters with bad manners and egos like trailer trucks, were sexist pigs. The expression must have been invented for them. There was one, you won't believe it, who was busy ordering a pair of chinos from L.L. Bean while I was there, sitting at his table, right across from him, and he asked me to measure the length of his pant leg from the crotch down so he'd be sure he got the right size! I walked out.

But getting back together with Thomas: you're right to ask about that. Probably it wouldn't have happened if my dunderhead brother John and Alex had kept their big fat mouths shut. Thomas was in the second year of business school. He went to the Harvard Club in New York for some sort of reception for business school students and important younger graduates, and saw Alex there. Alex asked him about me, and Thomas told him the truth: I'd stopped answering his letters, and he didn't know where I was or what I was doing. What he didn't tell Alex was that at the time he was himself seeing a Radcliffe junior, a Jewish girl from Brooklyn with a big nose and big tits, who'd take him in her mouth and tell him he was a great lover. If he had, perhaps Alex wouldn't have felt so sorry for Thomas. Instead, your *Lampoon* buddy said, That's terrible, we've got to do something about it. I'll ask old John De Bourgh what's going on and let you know. Your letters must have gone astray! Thomas says, Thank you very much, that's so good of you, Alex calls John, who gives him my address and telephone number, of course without bothering to ask whether I mind, and Alex gets on the phone to Thomas and says, You're in luck! I don't know whether it slipped John's mind or whether it was an attack of belated discretion: he didn't tell Alex about McLean or Dr. Reiner. I know John knew about McLean, because it was necessary to make arrangements with the trust company for paying the bills; I'm not sure he knew I was still in treatment. Next thing, there is Thomas waiting for me when I come home from Houghton Mifflin, right there in Louisburg Square, sitting on the stoop and reading some awful business-school book. He was so absorbed I could have walked on and hidden somewhere. Anywhere! As it was, I said hello. I have to admit, he was very clever. He didn't complain about my not writing, he didn't ask where I had been or even what I was doing, he just kept on repeating how glad he was to see me, how beautiful I was and how chic. It's a fact that I'd lost weight and had a very good haircut. Then he asked if he could take me out for tea or a drink. I think he said, Let's go to the Ritz. It was a five—ten—minute walk, and I was tired, so instead I asked him in. I offered him tea, although I really wanted a whiskey, because I didn't want to drink with him. Liquor seemed to go to my head more quickly, perhaps because of the medication I'd been on at McLean, and I wanted to remain self-possessed. I was also careful to tell him to sit down on the sofa and to sit down myself in the Queen Anne wing chair that had belonged to the same great-aunt who later left me the house in Little Compton. We drank the tea. I'd also put out some Pepperidge Farm cookies. It was all very peaceful until I put my teacup down. Right away he was on his knees before me, caressing my legs. I let him, although I hadn't shaved my legs, and there was bristle on the insides of my thighs. I hadn't been with anyone since Hubert walked out, and he got me very excited. I wasn't wearing stockings. He worked his hands under my skirt up to my waist, pulled off my panties and shoes, and pushed my legs apart. I thought it would be the old Harvard-boy routine. All those clubmen who'd stick a finger into you and churn and come in their pants, leaving you humiliated and furious. But he'd learned about female anatomy and actually made me come. Was he ever pleased! Lord knows from the very start I had tried to explain to him how it worked, but he just couldn't get it. Later he told me it was the girl from Brooklyn who'd taught him. When we finally made it to bed, he made me come the first time with him inside, and I remember telling him, Yes, this is the way. This is how you should always do it. Break me, break me like a mare.

Her own story had aroused her. I was certain it had. For

the first time that evening, there was color in her cheeks, and I am ashamed to admit to having felt myself a degree of unwholesome excitement. Before I could learn whether that incident had marked the resumption of their relationship and its progression toward marriage, the waiter brought the first course.

I shouldn't be telling you these things, she continued after a while, putting down her fork. They're so embarrassing. But otherwise you won't understand how it happened. They all work hard at the business school. Thomas had always been a good student. Perhaps he didn't have to work as hard as most others. Anyway he was constantly after me. Mostly wanting to fuck. Very soon after the first time he said very proudly that he'd told the Brooklyn girl about me, and that ended that. Perhaps he should have kept her; his performance stopped improving. It was the old story. One night I was so mad I got up and sat in the Queen Anne chair with a knit coverlet over my shoulders, shivering from cold. I was crying. He got out of bed too and said, Please stop, I'm going to make it all right. And he did. It was another useful trick the girl from Brooklyn taught him. A couple of men in France had showed me, and Hubert used to do it before he decided it was too much trouble, but I didn't think Thomas knew about such things. It drove me wild. Later we did variations on that theme that he really liked and I didn't. All I knew was that he was no Hubert. He wasn't a real man. It didn't help that when he came over in the evening—which was most evenings because he'd get his work done by the late afternoon—he wanted to spend the night and leave early enough to get to class on the MBTA. I couldn't allow that. The house belonged to the Mathers. Peter Mather taught Greek and ancient history at the college; both he and his wife were very stiff and agreed to rent the apartment to me only because they knew my family. I was sure that if they saw Thomas going out the door in the morning and hanging around on weekends all hell would break loose. They'd want me to leave. The argument over this went on and on. He'd insist, and apart from him and Dr. Reiner and my work with Emily, I had no one, nothing. I asked Dr. Reiner what I should do, and he said, You should do exactly as you wish. I thought about that advice and told Thomas I didn't think it was right to go on having an affair that tied me down and led to nowhere. All you and I do, I said, when we're not in bed is to go to your classmates' parties on football weekends, and all that happens there is they drink martinis and get smashed.

I knew his friends didn't know what to make of me. I was older and different from the girls they invited. At some point I asked Dr. Reiner whether he thought I could get married and have children. He said, You certainly are able to get married if that is what you really want to do, although normally it is best to avoid long-term commitments when one is in therapy, and he asked whether I had told Thomas I was in analysis. Because if you haven't, you might consider doing so. Thomas was a born snoop, and it was difficult to speak about my breakdown in Geneva and Dr. Reiner and leave out Hubert altogether, but I managed it by being vague. Anyway, I'm sure the last thing Thomas wanted was to understand. When I told Dr. Reiner I'd done what he'd said I should, I expected some sort of praise, a pat on the head, but it was just the usual *umm.* A short time afterward, Thomas refused to leave after we'd finished; I couldn't get him out of the apartment until the morning, and when I looked out the window I saw him and Professor Mather literally walking out of the house together. The next day when Thomas came over I yelled at him and told him we were through. If he wanted me he would have to marry me. I couldn't go on being his slut. He looked at me coldly, it was the first time I'd seen that, and asked, How can I marry you when you need to see your psychiatrist every day? I told him to get out. He didn't. Instead he practically raped me. If I hadn't let him do it, he'd have strangled me. When it was over he said he couldn't give me up, but before we talked about marriage he wanted to see Dr. Reiner.

I'll never forgive that bastard, she said after a moment of silence.

I assumed that she was referring to Thomas, but she made her meaning clear a moment later.

Can you believe it, she asked, he gave his word to Thomas that I was sound—that's the word he used—that marriage would be good for me, and that there was no reason I shouldn't have children? The next day I asked him how he could say such a thing after telling me I shouldn't make long-term commitments while I was in analysis. He looked at me, raised his eyebrows, and said that one's views change with circumstances. The conversation with Thomas had convinced him that this was my big chance for happiness!

VII

I WALKED LUCY HOME after dinner. Finding she was leaning on my arm more heavily than her doubtless very real fatigue justified, I declined the invitation to come upstairs for a nightcap. You needn't be afraid of me, she countered, and kissed me on the lips. I'm lonely but hardly dangerous. Come to see me soon. The truth was, however, that the rawness of her narration had made me uneasy: I felt I was being drawn closer to her than seemed wise and instinctively placed the blame on her. I knew that was unfair. She had spent years in analysis—she had said that she continued to see a psychoanalyst after she and Thomas moved to New York—learning how to speak explicitly about feelings and actions that were once, and perhaps still were, considered unmentionable, and I suspected she was still in some sort of therapy. Moreover, if I put aside habits she might have formed during all those years on the couch and looked at the problem strictly as a novelist, I had to ask myself a question to which I had no convincing answer: how else was she going to tell her story? It was also true that my curiosity, initially piqued by the gratuitous harshness of the way she had spoken about Thomas when we met at the ballet, had turned into something like an obsession. Prudence be damned: I was determined to understand how the quirky but beautiful, charming, and seductive young woman I had known had changed so, had become an embittered and aggressive shrew. It was a question that now greeted me each morning. Age and solitude had clearly done their work, but there had to be something else, a poison that she and Thomas had secreted. Was it possible that the guileless young man she had introduced to me more than half a century earlier, whom I had later known as a prominent and very successful financier credited with having made an important contribution to the resolution of the Latin American debt crisis, and, to use a sobriquet I dislike, a public intellectual of sorts, had been a monster in private life? More of a monster anyway than I and practically everyone else I could think of? So it happened that during the weeks that preceded her summer removal to Little Compton and mine to Sharon, I saw Lucy a number of times, at her apartment for tea—I had sworn to myself I would avoid having meals there—and over dinner in Jane's Lexington Avenue bistro that had become my East Side dining room.

I was impressed by her ability to keep the narrative going in chronological order, making it relatively easy to reconstruct as I thought about it later. The story developed relentlessly.

The very evening Thomas received Dr. Reiner's blessing

he came to her apartment carrying a bouquet of red roses and proposed. On bended knee. In her opinion, he was in fact terrified of the marriage that lay ahead and needed to commit himself to it quickly, burning his bridges. How was she to respond? She had set him on that path; she knew she needed to give shape to her life. Of course she said yes. Thereupon he called his parents, right from her apartment. She had assumed the parents would be over the moon when they heard that a De Bourgh had agreed to marry their son, but she was in for a surprise. They said—he had made the mistake of not telling them she was at his side, and both the mother and the father spoke loudly so that she heard every word—that he was too young, that he shouldn't get married until he had a job and was independent, and that this was a decision he would regret all his life. In subsequent conversations, all of which Thomas incomprehensibly repeated to her, they went after her, saying they could tell she was unsuitable for marriage and motherhood. At first she couldn't understand. What kind of gossip had they heard, why were plumbers, electricians, and pool men in Newport, the sort of people Snow *père et mère* consorted with, talking about her? Apart from one beach party she'd been to with Alex that had gotten out of hand and was broken up by the police she'd never done anything there that anyone could point a finger at. Then one day she understood: that idiot Thomas had told them that she was seeing a psychiatrist five days a week and was in analysis. That was more than enough for Mr. and Mrs. Snow. They got the picture. She was spoiled goods. On one level she had to hand it to the garage owner and the bookkeeper: they didn't let visions of De Bourgh money and social standing distract them from wanting their darling boy to find someone as perfect as he. They thought an unequal marriage would hurt him. On another level they made a big mistake. All that talk made Thomas dig in his heels. If there had ever been the slightest chance of getting him to back out of the engagement it was gone. Moreover, they had succeeded in giving her all the respectable reasons she needed not to have anything to do with them. Thomas would understand if she too dug in her heels and didn't want them in her house or near her and Thomas's children. Or if she relented, she would be doing him and them a big favor and would have every right to hold her nose.

Her own parents had not tried to see her or speak to her since she came back from Geneva. They certainly hadn't invited her to come home. Her only contacts with the family had been with her brother John—they talked on the phone every couple of weeks—and, over money, with her father's secretary, and that was hardly needed since her allowance came from her trust and she could deal with the trustee herself. Thomas wanted to get married in January, right after his final examinations, so they could get away from the Cambridge cold and spend a week in Puerto Rico. He must have meant by that, she said, that she would have the opportunity to take him on a honeymoon. He couldn't have afforded the airfare, never mind the hotel. Finally he agreed to postpone the wedding until sometime in early June, after his graduation. That was an easy decision. He didn't have a cent, and after what had happened he couldn't borrow from his parents. Waiting until after graduation brought them closer to the time when he would have a job and a salary. She had thought they'd simply get a marriage license and be pronounced man and wife at the city hall, with Dr. Reiner and whomever Thomas wanted among his classmates as witnesses. That was when Thomas's shameless arriviste side went on full display. He said, We must tell your parents, and, when she protested that she wasn't on speaking terms with them, he said, Don't worry about it, I'll write to them, and did so before she could stop him. Now you'll get your comeuppance, she told him, but once again she was wrong. Some days later, her father called and, sounding as though he had his mouth full of ice cubes, announced that her mother and he hadn't expected her to make such a good decision on such an important issue. Thomas was a fine young man, and they were happy to welcome him into the family. They understood that she and Thomas wanted to be married in June; that was fine, they'd be happy to have the wedding at the house in Bristol; he'd already told Thomas there would be a substantial wedding present in the form of money to help them get settled in their new life.

Then, she said, in early January, during the business-school reading period, right before Thomas's exams, I ran away, telling him I had to go to Paris to see about selling the apartment and the Mercedes. I'd talked about that before, and it represented a part of the truth. The other part, the real reason, was that I wanted to see Hubert. I'd called him the day before and said I was getting married and wanted to have one last good memory of our time together. The idea of my wanting to cheat on Thomas must have really turned him on.

There was this pause, and he said, Get a room at the Savoy in London, baby doll, *ma petite cocotte,* and wait for me there next Friday afternoon. In bed. Your legs open. As always, he made me melt. I sat down and masturbated. I knew his taste in hotels as well as sex, I knew I'd be picking up the tab each step of the way, and I didn't care. I reserved a small suite with a river view, which at the time, if you had dollars, wasn't such a big deal. Then in Paris, after signing stuff about the apartment and the car, I bought two Lanvin nightgowns and had my legs waxed at Elizabeth Arden, on place Vendôme. On Friday afternoon I was at the hotel in London, on the bed, my thighs open, ready for him.

I'll spare you the description of the kinky sex when he arrived. The next day, we had sat down to a late lunch downstairs at the Grill. Oysters and whiting and a lot of wine. He'd made me sore inside, but I liked that, and I was very happy to be on the banquette, leaning against him, feeling the warmth of his body. Something, probably the consciousness that I was being stared at, made me look up. Right away I saw who it was: Will Reading—in fact his father had just died, and he'd become Lord Reading—Thomas's business-school classmate and friend. He and another toff were at the table directly across from us. Why I hadn't noticed him before I'll never know, and there was no way I could have failed to recognize him. We'd met at parties, I'd danced with him, and he'd even tried to feel me up. He could tell that I'd finally seen him, gave me a horrid sort of wink, and came over to our table, kissed my hand the way that sort of Brit does, and just waited. I introduced them—there was no way to avoid it—and to my horror instead of keeping his mouth shut that idiot Hubert said, Oh, I'm charmed to meet one of my cousin Lucy's friends. My cousin Lucy! Hubert's accent had never been so thick. I knew that Will wouldn't resist the urge to tell Thomas; probably he believed it was his duty. The smirk on Will's face was really something. I couldn't get the thought that he'd already called Thomas leave my mind for a moment during what remained of that weekend, not during the orgasms or the tears when Hubert decided, after we had returned to the room after lunch, that he would whip me, something he had never tried before, saying, You have it coming to you, you bitch, *tu l'as bien mérité, salope.* The other thought that terrified me even more was that Dr. Reiner would no longer want me as a patient. I'd lied to him; I had told him I must go to Paris to take care of business and got him not to charge me for the missed sessions; he'd say I'd made continuing analysis with him impossible.

I was right about Will and Thomas; I was wrong about Dr. Reiner. Thomas called just as Hubert was leaving for the airport. He didn't shout; in this funny little voice he used when he was really mad he said, You're cheating, only a month after our engagement, and you're already cheating. I was still in bed, finishing my breakfast, and Hubert, instead of walking out the door, sat down on the side of the bed, put his hand under the covers, and tried to make me come, all the while making faces, a sort of commentary on what I was telling Thomas, and wouldn't take his hand away although I kept shaking my head and tried to close my legs tight. It came out that as soon as Thomas had heard from Will he had tried the Savoy, on the off chance, and had asked for me. Thank God the room was in my name! I lied and lied and lied. No wonder Hubert was amused.

She went on to say that she had told Thomas on the phone that the Swiss man she was having lunch with (she didn't reveal his name) was someone she had known years ago when she first came to Paris—she was smart enough not to say a word about Geneva—that it was all over between them, had been over for years, that he was working in London and was having difficulties at his job and in his marriage, that he had written to her, and that, since she was going to be in Paris anyway, she'd decided she really should see him and tell him in person that she was getting married. She'd wanted to say goodbye nicely. Thomas didn't believe her. That was perfectly clear. Finally she said, Please don't say or think things you'll be sorry about later. I will be in Boston on Thursday. Let's talk then. Of course he kept calling her every few hours until she checked out of the hotel, repeating, over and over, How could you have done such a thing? Then in Boston, at first he wouldn't see her. He told her there was no going back. It would be impossible to trust her, and the more he said that each time she called him, the more she begged him to reconsider. Meanwhile, Dr. Reiner astonished her by saying that what she had done with Hubert was an exorcism, her way of expelling the incubus, a necessary part of the progress toward coming to terms with herself. They resumed their daily sessions—naturally he changed tack and charged for the ten or so sessions she'd missed—and he encouraged her to persist with Thomas. He didn't think Thomas would accept the truth about the encounter with Hubert—but what was that truth?—and thought that rather than attempt to give him an account of those days she should work hard on demonstrating her commitment to him and to the marriage. By early spring she had succeeded—that was how Dr. Reiner saw it. The June date Thomas and she had picked for the wedding in Bristol fell directly after the Harvard commencement; the reception would be a small and modest affair—her family, inevitably his parents and a couple of aunts and uncles and cousins, some of his business-school friends, Will Reading not included, and a few close family friends and neighbors. Lucy tried to put her foot down when it came to the van Burens, who qualified as neighbors and friends; she really didn't want Priscilla or Alex, but in the end they were invited, as was I.

Thomas wanted you there, Lucy told me. You didn't come, I can't remember what excuse you gave, but you sent those lovely Georgian silver sugar tongs. The van Burens came, every single one of them, and gave us napkins. I swear it's true: tea-sandwich napkins!

But by that time it had also become evident that she would be unable to terminate the treatment with Dr. Reiner when his August vacation began and resume analysis or therapy in the fall with another doctor in New York. This was not Lucy's own idea, although the prospect of changing analysts had been terrifying her. It was Dr. Reiner himself, she told me, who said he couldn't take responsibility for ending her treatment at that time, not after all that had recently happened; he believed she should continue with him for at least one more year. He offered to see Thomas and tell him his opinion. Because Thomas, of course, was as usual thinking only of himself and his wonderful career and the offer he had accepted from Kidder Peabody of a job that started in the fall. Morgan Stanley hadn't made him an offer, although they'd made one to Josiah Weld. That had left Thomas speechless; he simply couldn't understand how such a thing could happen. His own record at the business school and at college was so much better, and he had the LSE degree. The reason was clear as a bell to Lucy, she told me, and she said she had explained it to him. You aren't white enough for Morgan, she said, and you never will be. One look at you and all they see is a striving townie. Afterward of course he invented the story that he preferred Kidder because he was going to work with Al Gordon.

That was that. It didn't occur to Thomas to say to Kidder he wouldn't be starting work in the fall and ask for a deferment of the offer, but he did offer to commute to Boston on weekends. Her answer was that if they weren't going to live together the wedding was off; if he wanted her, he had better take a job on State Street. They could get a larger place on Beacon Hill, and he could walk to work. He absolutely refused.

Somewhere at that point I interrupted and said, Once again you had an opportunity to postpone a marriage you were so ambivalent about, or to back out from it altogether, handed to you on a silver platter. Why didn't you?

She shook her head and told me she didn't know. She hadn't been well. Dr. Reiner had been in favor of the marriage. Now he talked about her going back to McLean. What would happen to her if she broke with Thomas? If she did marry him, yes, it would be a relief to have him in Boston only on weekends—anyway, those weekends when he could make it; it certainly wouldn't be every weekend; she knew that Kidder worked its young people hard. But she didn't trust him; he was oversexed; he'd pick up gonorrhea or worse from some slut and give it to her. She'd be terrified to let him near her. Besides, where would he live in the city? He had no one he could stay with; she'd end up paying his rent. He had been quite insulting about working on State Street. Boston was a backwater, no better than Providence; even a year or two of work for a State Street bank would tarnish his résumé and spoil his prospects on Wall Street. Dr. Reiner said she should in fact encourage Thomas to commute. She'd get the emotional space she needed, and it was more sensible to spend money on separate establishments than to push Thomas to take a job he didn't want. He also said her fears of whores and infections weren't reasonable. I don't know what I should have done, Lucy said. I was tired of spending money; I was tired of Thomas; I was tired of Dr. Reiner; I was tired of everything and everybody. Thereupon, out of the blue, Thomas talked the business school into giving him a junior faculty position and a fellowship to do research on valuation theory, both good for two years. In a way it wasn't all that surprising. He was right at the top of his class, and he'd become close to the professor directing the research. Kidder made no difficulties about delaying his arrival. Al Gordon even called and said he was thrilled by this recognition of

Thomas's merit. Can you imagine the stupidity of that man? Dr. Reiner was impressed. As for Thomas, his head was turned. He never recovered. Only got worse and worse. He could do no wrong; his work naturally came ahead of everything else; he had to be the center of attention. He actually wrote to my father, Lucy said, about the faculty appointment—when he told me about it I exploded, but he said he'd done it because he knew my father would be proud of him and would be pleased to have the news come from him directly. My poor father responded by sending him a check for a thousand dollars. I was mortified; I could just hear Mother making fun of Thomas. She could be so mean. My idiot brother John also took Thomas seriously, just like Father. It's the stupidity gene of De Bourgh males. The wedding was a couple of weeks later, Lucy said. I went through the reception more dead than alive. Dr. Reiner didn't want me to be away for more than a week or ten days. Attending the wedding was too much for my great-aunt—she hardly left her apartment on Pinckney Street in Boston anymore—but she told me to treat the house in Little Compton as though it were my own, although she'd go on taking care of the taxes and upkeep. That's where we went directly from the reception.

VIII

I HAD TAKEN to seeing Lucy almost daily, in the afternoon at her apartment over tea or at dinner at the Lexington Avenue bistro. The uneasiness her narration had caused me had dissipated, but for a variety of reasons, including my desire to avoid late evenings and excessive consumption of alcohol, I stuck to my resolution to decline invitations to drinks or to dinner at her place. Occasionally, we took advantage of the fine weather and talked in the afternoon on a bench facing the Central Park boat basin. One day in the park, she asked me point-blank, and with only the thinnest smile, whether I was writing a book about her and Thomas. Was that the purpose of our interviews? Wasn't that what they really were, ever since I first came to dinner at her house? I told her the truth: I was working on something quite different, a novel set in my native Salem, but after I had finished, if I lived long enough and hadn't lost my marbles, I might want to write a book about the breakup of a marriage. A marriage, I stressed, a fictional character's marriage, not hers and Thomas's. Naturally, everything I learned in the course of our talks would be part of my experience and my store of knowledge and observations and could have an impact on the story I'd tell. But the book would be a novel, not a memoir or reportage.

A novel. She snorted. And you'll put me and what I've told you into it. I'll murder you!

That's one of the hazards of a novelist's profession, I answered, just as finding some aspects of yourself in a novel is a risk you run by palling around with a novelist—or merely allowing yourself to be in his field of vision.

She wasn't laughing, so I added that if I did write the book neither she nor anyone else would recognize her or Thomas in my characters or have grounds to argue that the book was about them. They'd be seeing a mosaic, made of slivers of glass or stone, some picked up as I went along and some I had fabricated. I don't write romans à clef, I said.

She snorted again and to my great relief kept talking. Our conversations continued over what remained of that week and much of the following week, with time out for the weekend, about which I told her a fib. I said I would be visiting my ailing cousin Hetty in Philadelphia. In reality, I had accepted an invitation from Jane Morgan to spend the weekend with her and her husband in Water Mill, getting wind of which, I hadn't a doubt, would send Lucy into orbit. As I had expected, the information Jane was to give me proved precious.

Getting married, setting up a real household, not feeling adrift, Lucy said, that was in some ways what I had always wanted. At the same time, after that awful wedding—it wasn't objectively awful, nothing at that house could be; it just felt that way—and that monstrous honeymoon in Little Compton, I returned to Boston knowing I was in a trap. One I had set myself and couldn't get out of! Can you imagine it—Mr. and Mrs. Snow declared that they wanted to call on us in Little Compton and bring things for the house, which turned out to be homemade jams and tomato chutneys, and Thomas insisted that we must receive them? He didn't want to break their hearts! He didn't want to burn his bridges! They'd worked so hard! And my heart? I don't think he took it into consideration. He'd already decided, and you can be sure that his parents were directing his thoughts, that I wasn't fully rational, so that if he wanted to do this or that against my will the thing to do was to badger me into accepting it. Going along. Having Mr. and Mrs. Snow to tea served on my great-aunt Helen's best china and best tablecloth. The trust company found the larger apartment we needed on the top floor of a building on Beacon Street across from the Public Garden. It was where Alan Crawford, who taught Renaissance Italian literature, and his wife lived. I'd taken his seminar, and he gave me an A. After the start of the school year, they had us over to dinner once and twice to drinks. I think that Thomas bored Alan, but I could see that Alan was contemplating making a play for me. Living in the same building would have made getting together convenient, and I wouldn't have minded, but he chickened out. Perhaps Susan, that was his wife, sensed what was going on and read him the riot act. Other than my place on rue Casimir-Perier, which you surely remember, it was the nicest apartment I've ever lived in. Sunny and well proportioned, and with a beautiful view. I could walk to work. But as soon as Dr. Reiner left for his Wellfleet vacation I realized I really wasn't well at all; I knew I was sinking. Thomas would come home late; he was doing research in the library. He had this idea that when he walked through the door the table should be set, and as soon as he'd washed his hands we should have a drink, which was an idea he'd picked up from me, and sit down and eat. Of course, I was supposed to have the dinner ready, at most it would need to be reheated, that's all. I couldn't do that. Why should it be me who set the table, who did the shopping, who cooked? We fought about that. Over and over. Shopping wasn't easy—I had to go all the way to Charles Street. I could order by phone from one fancy market and have whatever it was delivered, but that meant I didn't see the fruit or the lettuce, and anyway I had to be at home when the order arrived. We didn't have a doorman. It was a hot August, the way it can be hot and muggy in Boston. In the streets it was brutal, but even so the apartment was pleasant. You'd think he would have wanted to take a bath or shower when he came home, before we had drinks, and have dinner late when you could open the windows and get some breeze, but no, that wasn't how it should be; the garage owner washed to get the grease off, but Thomas hadn't spent his day under some car putting in a new exhaust pipe. It was all I could do to get Thomas to take a shower before he went to bed! And to stop him from sitting down to dinner in his shirtsleeves and necktie. He'd tuck his necktie into his shirt! You have to live with someone to realize you can't stand them. We hadn't tried to live together before, the trip to Italy didn't count, and now I knew I couldn't abide him. Oh, of course, he could be taught. Once it had sunk in that in Bristol, even when my father and mother dined alone, Father would put on his green or plum velvet smoking jacket and a foulard or black tie, and Mother a long skirt, and that changing before dinner into something—anything—was what one did, wild horses couldn't have dragged him to the table in the clothes he'd worn when he came in from the street, and I thought that the willingness to conform was revolting too, so craven, so unnatural. But the stuff about doing his share in the house, there was nothing to be done; the roots had sunk too deep. It was the importance of his work. When he came home from work, everything was supposed to be nice. For him! So he had the right atmosphere to do whatever he was doing. It didn't help that my boss Emily was on vacation, and I had to go over manuscripts at home just to keep up.

It got worse when classes at the business school started and he had to prepare the course he was teaching in addition to doing the research. You'd think he deserved a medal, because everything he did was so special and he was doing it all so well. Meanwhile I was trying to fix Jerzy Kosinski's manuscript, and that was difficult not only because I was putting it into real English but also because Emily was stuck on the idea that it was basically a true account of what had happened to him during the war in Poland that should be published as a memoir and wouldn't back off, even though it was clear, if you asked questions about it without spooking

Jerzy, that the book was a brilliant, inspired invention that could only be published as a novel. The truth is that Jerzy liked me. Not only the way most men usually did, thinking of sex, but because of how I helped with the manuscript. There was nothing between us, but when Thomas finally met Jerzy at Emily's he went into one of his lockjaw-and-withdrawal routines, hardly able to speak, because right away he had sensed the attraction. Of course, Jerzy saw exactly what was going on and picked on him. That happened every time he and Thomas were together, and it was too bad because when we moved to New York, Jerzy was one of the very few interesting people we knew, and through him we could have met everybody.

For a while I tried hard to create a world for us away from the business school and Thomas's colleagues. Most of them were dreary, and the ones who weren't liked me, but when they did Thomas would act like a spoiled brat or make a scene after they left if we had them over or when we came home from wherever we had been. I got in touch with some Radcliffe classmates living in Boston or the suburbs. One had also been at Farmington with me. I had the idea that old friendships could be revived. Since I felt constantly drained from fatigue, it wasn't an easy thing to do, but I made the effort. The response of a couple of them—one living in Dover and the other in Cambridge—was wonderful. It made me remember that being Lucy De Bourgh had its good sides. They genuinely wanted to see me, to meet Thomas, to introduce us to their friends. But after a weekend dinner or lunch at their house, followed by a meal at our apartment or at an Italian restaurant in the North End, I could see it was no use. They'd gotten married soon after graduation to men a few years older. One was a lawyer. The other was working for Raytheon in some scientific capacity. They'd all had proper weddings with nice Shreve and Crump invitations, bridesmaids, and ushers; they had children in kindergarten or first or second grade; they played indoor tennis. The men had sloops they kept in Marblehead. If the weather was right, they sailed on weekends. For summer vacation they'd take their boats up to Maine to stay with parents on Mount Desert, where the whole clan would gather. It was the same story with my Borden and Hubbard cousins in Boston. They liked Thomas all right, whatever that meant, perhaps he amused them, but he didn't sail, he didn't ski, he was younger, and he was self-important. There was no place for him when they got their friends together on Saturday evening to dance to records. Or for me. The wives, perhaps the men too, sensed that something had gone wrong with me. What had come of all that time I had spent in Paris, hadn't there been a problem at Farmington, although they couldn't remember just what it was about, was there trouble between my parents and me, where had I found Thomas and who was he anyway, why hadn't they been invited to our wedding, had we in fact been married in Bristol? You can imagine this sort of thing. My old classmates and cousins with their well-run lives, their routine of dinner parties, and once a month, or however often it came, time to twirl around the dance floor at the waltz evening. My cousin Bessie actually invited us twice. Thomas didn't have tails, but that was all right, he wore his dinner jacket, which he'd bought alone so it had the wrong cut and anyway didn't fit. The real problem was that he didn't know how to waltz. He hardly knew how to dance! Where would he have learned? I didn't try to teach him. It was pointless, because you really had to dance very well or on that floor you were a nuisance. I liked to waltz, I liked those evenings, and whether Thomas knew how to dance or didn't made no real difference. But Bessie stopped inviting us. Perhaps this wasn't a new development, but the truth is that I was only then becoming aware of a simple fact. Lucy De Bourgh was *déclassée*, no longer someone you kept on your list once you had them on it. On top of that, I was less and less well. Dr. Reiner didn't think I was making a sufficient effort during our sessions; once more he talked of sending me back to McLean; he had me evaluated by a colleague on Marlborough Street, an awful man who talked of trying an electroshock treatment. I escaped from his office in tears. The next day when I saw Dr. Reiner he said the Marlborough Street man should have perhaps explained how far ECT had progressed and that it was only one of several possible therapies. Nevertheless, I should be aware that he, Dr. Reiner, considered our failure to move forward troubling; he was taking it very seriously. He asked questions about my work, which was actually the only thing in my life going well, and as usual about Thomas. I told him the truth. The marriage had been a mistake; I disliked Thomas; I was sinking into a bog. Dr. Reiner had no answer. He was wrecking my life and emptying my bank account pretending to look for one.

She began to cry, for the first time since our first meetings.

We were sitting on a park bench. I put my arm around her shoulder and patted her, unable to find words of comfort.

That's all right, she said, thank you. Or no, it's not all right. You know how they fuck you up, your mom and dad, they don't mean to, but they do? Of course, you do. They sure fucked me up, or if it wasn't them it was the men who had used me, Thomas included, or all those goddamn De Bourghs and Goddards who had handed down the wrong genes. I have not had the life I had expected. I'm sure I've told you that ten times already, but saying it again doesn't make it less true. Or the life I deserved. Anyway, even Thomas could tell I was sick. He asked what Dr. Reiner advised me to do. I lied and said he was sending me back to McLean. I'd never told him about having already been in that place, after I returned from Geneva, so this came as a jolt. He knew I was damaged goods, but now he really knew he'd married a crazy woman. Probably he was scared, and he offered to go to see Dr. Reiner and talk about what should be done. I said he didn't need to bother. There was nothing Dr. Reiner could do for me beyond taking my money and writing prescriptions. I knew better than anyone else what I needed: it was to change the way I lived. Otherwise I'd break. He could count on it. They'd lock me up for good.

That night, when we were in bed, and I was going to get up and put in the diaphragm, he said, Don't. Let's make a child. That's the change in your life you need. You'll see. You'll be happy and you'll be well. All the while he was touching me just the way I had told him he should, and as I came I had a vision of what a baby of my own would be like, how I would love it, how I would do everything to make sure everything was right for him, a vision that was so strong that I said, Yes, do it, and drew him inside me. We fucked all night. I don't know how many times he came. The crazy thing is that I didn't get pregnant right away. I had my period, and then another and yet another. Finally I missed a period and had the test. The child was there. And during all that time, I talked to Dr. Reiner about it and what it would be like to have the baby and bring it up and how everything would turn out well, and he let me babble on like that and never said the one and only sensible thing, which was that a child has never fixed a bad marriage or cured someone like me. Of course, Thomas and I should have known that ourselves or should have gotten different and better advice. So Jamie was born, and he was the most beautiful child, the most perfect beautiful little man anyone had ever seen, and he was a very good boy too. Then I had two miscarriages, one after another. Why were we trying to have another child? We'd gotten used to doing it without a diaphragm. He liked it, and I did too. Then the depression settled down on me heavier than ever. Do you understand now? Do you see how idiotic it is to talk of me working? I was in bad shape when we moved to New York. The apartment was freshly wallpapered, the curtains were new, but I was in tatters. That's how you saw me on your first visit.

I said that if that had been the case she had put on a very good show.

The memory of your complaining about the apartment being north of Seventy-Second Street and on the wrong side of the avenue and so forth, I told her, had made me wonder for a moment whether you'd just stepped out of a Peter Arno cartoon, but otherwise? You and Thomas had seemed the epitome of a young Wall Street investment banker and his *Mayflower*- or *Arabella*-descendant wife, a picture only enhanced when the nurse brought in Jamie, and he was scurrying around the living room in his Carter's pajamas with feet.

I'm glad you thought so, she replied scowling. For your information, my Warren cousins came on the *Mayflower* and my Dudley cousins on the *Arabella*. The De Bourghs and the Goddards were latecomers. Whatever kind of impression we may have made on you, life was pure hell, and it got worse. I did have a new doctor who was really quite helpful, at least in the beginning, and the nurse, the one who looked like Aunt Jemima, was very good, the best we ever had. But she quit; she couldn't stand hearing Thomas and me fight. I was lonely, I was wretched, and when I finally met people I liked through Penny Stone, who'd come back from Paris and was living in New York—you probably remember her, she was a photo model then—Thomas was odious about them. There were some others, the old crowd. A faggot poet I'd known in Paris who double-crossed me later, a painter. People who had talent and were beginning to be recognized and anyway knew how to be amusing. Thomas put the kibosh on it. It was just the way he had been with Jerzy! He said they were louche; the fact is that he felt threatened by them. He wanted to be with society people, you know, friends of my parents, distant cousins, and so on, or with his colleagues and clients. That all changed, of course, when he became a big deal and started to move in intellectual circles with all the people who he was goddamn sure mattered. But that was later, after we'd split up, once he'd teamed up with that dreadful Jane Morgan!

There was no way she could realize it, but she'd just given me the opening I needed.

You mean after you got him to agree to a divorce, I asked.

He was a cheat, she answered, a very clever, slippery cheat. You can't imagine how tired it made me. I should have asked for a divorce a hundred times. Each time I said, I know what you're doing, he'd put on this dumb blank expression or fly into a rage. He'd say, If I have done something wrong and you can prove it, tell me about it, and I'll tell you whether it's true or not, I'll give you all the explanations you want, I'll admit what's true, but don't you dare accuse me of things you can't prove. I was afraid of him, afraid that he'd kill me. Of course, I couldn't prove any of it, he was far too sneaky and careful, but that didn't matter to me. I just knew. My intuition has never been wrong. One way I could tell was that he wanted new kinds of sex. He'd try them on me, usually when I was almost asleep. Somebody was showing him things I swear he hadn't known, and he missed them when he was with me. If I said, Why are you doing this, it's not what married couples do, not unless normal sex no longer works for them, he had the effrontery to claim he was only doing what he had noticed really excited me. Finally I realized what was going on: it wasn't sluts he paid or the pornography he was watching on Eighth Avenue. I knew all about that; he'd made me sit through *Deep Throat* and *Behind the Green Door.* It was Jane Morgan. Why else were we with the two of them all the time, her and that awful husband Horace she threw over as soon as she knew she'd harpooned Thomas? There was no other reason. Other lawyers at that firm and other law firms worked for Thomas, and he wasn't always asking them and their wives to dinner with him and me at this or that restaurant. He just had to be with her. It didn't matter whether I or that man were there too. I even caught them playing footsie under the table. I talked to my doctor about it, and he said, If that is so, you should consider bringing that relationship into the open and making everybody assume their responsibilities. I did just that. I called Horace at his office and said, There is this one little thing you should know: your great friend and client, Mr. Thomas Snow, is fucking your wife. Perhaps you need to talk to her about it. He hung up on me without saying a word, and when I called back his secretary said he was in a meeting and couldn't be disturbed. No wonder. See no evil, hear no evil: he didn't want to know anything that would complicate his relations with his most important client, perhaps even get him fired. So the next day in the morning, just as Thomas was setting out for the office, I told him what I had done, and I could tell that I had really gotten to him, right where it hurt. He turned white and left the apartment without one word. I supposed he'd come home in the evening and get violent. He'd hit me earlier that month over nothing. He'd taken a table at the Metropolitan Museum dinner where Al Gordon was being honored, he'd invited some of his usual business friends, including of course the loathsome Jane and her husband, I'd said I'd go, and then something happened to me. I was all dressed up, but I couldn't go, I couldn't leave the house; I sat down on the floor and screamed. All right, he'd have to rearrange the seating at his table, but otherwise it wasn't a big deal. He said, Stop this noise or I'll call your doctor. I didn't stop, I didn't even want to. All right, he told me. I'm making that call. I got there before he did. It was a telephone connected to the jack by a very long wire, so we could move it around the living room. I threw it at him hard, aiming at his chest. But it was a bad throw; it hit him in the face. He checked whether his nose was bleeding—of course it wasn't, it had just cut his lip—and then slapped me, really hard; it left a red mark on my cheek. So you can see, I had reason to be scared.

But he came back to the apartment much earlier, in the midafternoon. I was in the library. He didn't say a word. I didn't either. In a few minutes I saw him with a suitcase in hand. He must have gone to the closet where we kept them. This time I followed him as he carried it into the bedroom, and he threw in his toilet kit, photos of Jamie from the top of his dresser, and a suit. Perhaps some shirts and stuff like that. All in perfect silence while I watched. As soon as he'd finished he went into Jamie's room. Again, I followed. Jamie was just finishing his homework, and Hugh Cowles, the St. Bernard's master who worked with him in the afternoons, was leaving. Thomas said goodbye to Hugh in his normal voice. Those were the first words I'd heard him speak since he came home. Then the moment Hugh was out the door, that monster told Jamie he wasn't going to live with us at the apartment anymore, but they would see each other a lot, and some other nonsense of that sort, and anyway once Jamie got to Exeter in the fall it would be a whole other ball game. Jamie wasn't to worry. How did the monster know I'd let him near the kid? As you can imagine, Jamie cried, and when Thomas tried to shush him he said—I'll never forget Jamie's saying that, he was such a good kid at the time—I love you, Daddy, I so wish you would stay with Mommy and me!

I can't remember what kind of answer Thomas gave. He picked up his suitcase and walked out without one word for me. I didn't even know where he was going. Later his secretary called to say that he could be reached at the Plaza, but only—I still remember the thrill in her voice when she said it, that woman hated me so—in case of a real emergency. Can you believe it? That bastard never came back to the apartment, didn't even clear out his stuff. Maybe a month later, when his secretary called to give me his address and telephone number at an apartment he'd gotten on Seventy-Third Street, I said I would have all of it put in boxes and sent to him if he paid the mover. She said she'd check and get back to me. She did, the next day. Mr. Snow suggested that I have the rear-elevator man get rid of whatever I didn't want for my personal use.

We had been talking over tea at her apartment, and I found that being there, as it were, on the scene helped me visualize the events she had described. As one might expect, she was upset, and so was I, and I broke my self-imposed rule and asked her whether we could have a drink of something stronger than tea.

You know where to find the liquor, she told me.

I got us our usual whiskeys, and we drank them in companionable silence, which I broke to ask another question, this one I thought certain to provoke her.

Did he slap as hard as Hubert?

She surprised me by laughing. No, Thomas was always a wimp and a sissy.

I took a moment to absorb that and told her that in two days I would move to Sharon for the rest of the summer.

Well, I guess you've gotten what you wanted, she replied, so now you don't need to hang around. That seems to be the pattern in my life. Men help themselves to whatever I have and leave slamming the door behind them. Only you'd never do anything so unequivocal; you'll tiptoe out and shut the door ever so gently.

I was about to protest, but she held up her hand and added, Don't worry, I'm not mad at you, I'm leaving for Little Compton tomorrow. Peter and Mary Chaplin are giving a housewarming. They've sold the big house and are moving into a very nice cottage near the club. But if I get bored, or there is too much fog over the water, I may just come to see you in Connecticut. Let's make sure I have the right telephone number.

IX

A S I HAVE mentioned before, the weekend I had told Lucy I'd be spending with my aged cousin Hetty in Philadelphia I had spent in fact in Water Mill, with Jane Morgan and Ned Morris, her new husband. I took the train to Southampton on Saturday morning, Jane picked me up at the station, and we got to her house in time for a late lunch. It was my first visit to the house, although Thomas had talked about it often. All I knew about the new husband was that Thomas had brought him into his firm as a partner a few years before he retired and cashed out. The house turned out to be a rambling white clapboard affair on Flying Point Road set in an overgrown garden that ended at a salt marsh. Beyond it lay the ocean. Poor Thomas loved this place, Jane said, with all its imperfections. All the funny-shaped rooms one can't possibly use, the four porches, the way everything new you bring into it is instantly absorbed. Armchairs and sofas that you've just had reupholstered, curtains that were sewn and hung last week look as though they had been here since the beginning of time. He bought it and had it renovated before we decided to get married. He used to say it was the house he'd always wanted, and it's impossible not to feel his presence here. Knowing this you'll probably ask yourself why Ned and I decided to live here. I guess the answer is that we like it too, a lot. Jamie didn't want it—he doesn't plan to spend time on the East Coast—and neither he nor I wanted to put it on the market, so Ned bought it from the estate. Jamie's been out here since and says he feels good about it. I can tell what you're thinking: the apartment in New York. Thomas left it to me and I saw no need to move.

Poor Thomas indeed! I did not tell her that having been able to buy the Water Mill house and get it to be just so must have been the fulfillment of the fondest of his Walter Mitty dreams. Perhaps she realized it. Instead, I said that my house in Sharon, although smaller than this one, had many of the same characteristics.

We found Jane's husband in his study, doing what I suppose big-time investment bankers like to do on weekends: he was on the phone with a client in Moscow. While Jane performed a pantomime designed to put an end to the call, I examined him. He was, I guessed, a good fifteen years younger than Thomas, tall and massive, with a Li'l Abner face and big freckled hands that I could imagine gripping the putter with such force that the knuckles turned white as he prepared to birdie the hole. A look around the study confirmed my intuition. It was a storehouse of tournament mementos, golfing knickknacks, photographs of Ned with ruddy-faced men who I assumed were ranking players, golf clubs, and golf bags ancient enough to call for decommissioning. Was Ned happier multiplying his millions or on the links? Did it matter, given his great looks, the fortune he already possessed, and the air of having the world by the tail? What a change it was from Thomas, who'd never learned the game, and after he discovered the treadmill at the gym where he offered his employees and colleagues subscriptions had even given up his daily run in Central Park.

At last Ned put down the telephone and assured me of his long-standing desire to meet the great novelist who had also been a dear friend of his late mentor and partner. Seeing that Jane had already gotten me a gin and tonic and was bringing him what looked like bourbon on the rocks, he announced that we had better take our drinks to the table. His conference call would resume in a little more than an hour. I was glad to see that the table was set on a screened porch and that waiting on it were cold lobsters. Although they were split down the middle, and the claws were cracked, they demanded our attention, and it was some minutes before we turned to the number one political subject of the moment, the simmering preparations for the reelection campaign of 2004.

I said to Ned that Jane had told me he knew Senator Kerry. What do you think of him? I asked.

Ned laughed. A war hero, a truly courageous antiwar activist, a great politician. And a great guy. I'm for him, and I'm doing all I can to be useful. I'm even a fan of Teresa's. Of course, I also knew and liked the first husband. The right kind of Republican. I don't know whether Jane has told you, but I'm from Pittsburgh, or rather a suburb. Sewickley. My family has known the Heinzes forever. We were always asked to their Christmas parties. Jane has told me you'd like to help jazz up the campaign but have had trouble getting through to the right people. I'll see what I can do to establish contact.

We had thrown the lobster shells and carcasses onto what Jane called the bone plate, we had finished an oak leaf lettuce salad, and I had drunk glass after glass of white wine. I had found the food and drink excellent, and it had become very clear to me that I liked Ned, that he and Jane were a good couple, the kind of couple that makes others comfortable and happy. I felt a pang of envy as I thought of a time, not so very long ago, when Bella and I served to friends on our porch in Sharon lunches that, in their Gallic way, were just as good.

A young woman cleared the dishes and returned with dessert plates and a huge bowl of strawberries. Local farmer's hothouse, Jane remarked. On her next trip the young woman brought sugar cookies that tasted homemade. I complimented Jane on them. She smiled, and Ned refilled my glass. My head was beginning to turn, but I made no move to stop him.

Shall we all have coffee? Jane asked, and turning to Ned said, If you need to get back to your oligarchs before they zoom off to their dachas I'll bring your coffee to your study.

That would be good, he answered. I'll take a look at my notes before making the call.

What a nice man, I said when she returned. I'm truly grateful for this opportunity to meet him. Is there any coffee left? As you can probably tell, I'm a little tipsy.

She refilled my cup and patted my hand.

Yes, he's a very nice man, she said. He's even better than that. Here, have another sip of coffee. If you feel up to it, I'll take you for a walk.

The beach was just as I remembered it from a time when Bella and I used to stay with friends in East Hampton: white, seemingly endless, and, even on this gorgeous June Saturday, deserted except for a scattering of fathers playing racquet games with their children near the entrance to the parking lot. We walked briskly, Jane setting the pace, and, although the sand was hard and smooth, after a half hour of trotting at her side I began to wonder how much longer I could keep up. She may have sensed my fatigue and said, Let's turn back. We don't want to find we're in Montauk. The return was easier, but when we reached Water Mill, I was grateful for her suggestion that we sit down at the edge of the dune and relax.

Look, she said abruptly, I want to get some things off my chest. I can't help wondering what kind of poison Lucy's been feeding you during your visits. Probably I shouldn't care. There will never be a biography, but the record has been made, and it's one to be proud of. Thomas would have liked the obituary in the *Times*. It made the first page under the fold, there were no mistakes, and the tone was just right. The people in his firm adored him. So did his clients, especially all those Mexican and Latin American finance ministers and central bankers. So did everybody who worked for him later at his foundation, and I believe the same is true of the think tanks he collaborated with and places like the Council on Foreign Relations. But you remember what Mark Antony says: "The evil men do lives after them; / The good is oft interred with their bones." True or not, it's cynical and ghastly. I'd like to think that the good that Thomas did will live for a while. He did quite a lot of good—quietly, because he was shy. He did no evil; I'm certain of that. I've never seen or heard of any act that was malicious or intended to harm. He was his own most severe critic. The instance that will interest you is his conviction that he'd acted irresponsibly—he'd been criminally negligent is what he said—when he married Lucy, because deep inside he knew that the marriage would be a wreck, and again when he told her he wanted them to have a child, because he should have realized how hard it would be to have such parents. The worst part, according to him, was the unfairness of how it all turned out. He came through unscathed. I don't mind saying it—we had a very happy life together. As for his professional success, there is no need to talk about it. He made a great deal of money. That was not unimportant to him. We both know about Lucy. Of course, he realized that she had had serious problems before the marriage, but even so he couldn't get out of his mind how much better off she might have been with a very different man. For instance, one who had enough authority to make her toe the line. I'd tell him he was nuts. She would have murdered anyone who tried that. The miracle, so far as he was concerned, was that Jamie had turned out so well and that their relationship was so good. Thomas adored him. I'm sorry, I realize I've been rambling. The point I'm trying to make, though, is in fact simple: he valued you and liked you a lot. If there are blanks in the picture you have of Thomas, I think he deserves better than to have them all filled in by Lucy.

At least the marriage to this lady was entered into soberly and advisedly, I said to myself, and felt uneasy about returning to the subject of the failed marriage. But she had as much as urged me to ask questions. I decided to take her at her word.

There is a blank, I said, that puzzles me. Because of Jamie, if for no other reason, leaving Lucy must have been very painful. How old was Jamie? Thirteen? Fourteen? The marriage had been rocky practically from the beginning. You volunteered, when we had lunch in the city, that you were not the reason he left and that I shouldn't believe Lucy if she claimed otherwise. She does; she says he left her for you, and she's rather colorful about it. But if that is wrong, why did he leave? Why then? Why not after Jamie had gone to boarding school? Or earlier, before they had him?

You're right, she replied. Leaving Jamie had been very hard for Thomas and very hard on Jamie. Thomas said that seeing him cry when he told him he was leaving was the most painful moment of his life. The strange fact is that I don't know why he left at that particular time, although I knew and practically everyone around them realized the marriage was rocky. I really don't. He refused to tell me, saying that he left because he had to and didn't want to talk about it; the circumstances concerned no one except Lucy and him. I saw no reason to press him. Does Jamie know? I have no idea; he hasn't said so since his father died, and I wouldn't dream of asking. One person other than Lucy who does know is your old college friend Alex van Buren. Thomas let that slip. Don't you think that's odd? The only explanation that has occurred to me is that when it happened he was under great stress and really had to tell someone, and he was very attached to Alex. The summer jobs at Alex's parents' place in Newport and the connection to that whole family had meant a great deal to him. Perhaps Alex will be willing to tell you. If he does, I'd just as soon not hear what you find out.

I got back to the city on Sunday evening, called Alex and found that he and Priscilla had also just returned from Long Island, in their case from the North Shore. When I asked whether there was a time when it would be convenient for him to see me, he replied, Why not tomorrow? At the Paddock. Twelve-thirty. No, you're much too young, he told me, brushing off the suggestion that I take him to lunch. Besides, he continued, I've already written to the admissions committee about you, and Josiah has seconded the proposal. It's a good thing for you to show your face to the boys. We'll have you in the club before Christmas.

Just as I had feared, Alex wasted half an hour or more introducing me to a collection of regulars at the bar and extolling the qualities that would make me a feather in the club's cap. Consequently, when we had finished our drinks and finally sat down at the far end of the long table, where miraculously we were alone, I didn't hesitate to get directly to the point.

The chance encounter with Lucy at the ballet, I said, so

soon after my return to the city, stirred a cauldron of dormant old memories, and the image of the girl she had been when I got to know her in Paris became very vivid. I'm not sure whether I've told you that I met Thomas Snow through her, also in Paris; in fact she brought him to my apartment in order to introduce him to me. Thomas and I became friends, from the very beginning. We've all changed, but she has changed in ways that astound me. I can't attribute them only, or even principally, to aging. The old Lucy—the funny, original, devil-may-care girl I knew quite well in Paris—has quite simply disappeared. Or rather I have momentary, very brief glimpses of her once in a while, like those of an injured ghost. She isn't unconscious of the change, and to her mind Thomas is responsible for much, perhaps most, of the ravage. She is very bitter and hostile. I'm struck by the fact that a lot of what she complains about—how she was always giving and he was only taking, how she never got anything back— is a matter of her bad timing. She didn't remain with him until the time came to bring in the harvest. You know what I mean: success, money, position. Just as those good things were going to happen or had started happening, he stormed out. She's made it clear that it was he who left, in a great huff. Why? Why at that time? If I am to believe what she says, the marriage had been in real trouble for a long time, practically from the start.

Alex nodded but remained silent.

I'm glad you agree about that, I said. Bella and I thought that, but we had no insight into what went on between them, and Thomas, whom I kept seeing right up to the end, never discussed his life with Lucy. In fact, he gave me the strong impression that questions about it would be unwelcome. He did talk about Jamie.

Alex nodded again and said, So Lucy has been brainwashing you. Or rather stuffing you with what is for you new information.

She's trying to, I told him, and that's one of the many reasons I've asked to see you. I believe you know Thomas's second wife, Jane Morgan, and her current husband, Ned Morris. It so happens that I was staying with them in Water Mill over this past weekend. Jane talked to me about Thomas and her desire to protect his memory from slander. She returned with considerable emphasis to something she had told me a couple of weeks earlier—namely, that Thomas did not leave Lucy for her. By the way, that such was the reason is the gist of Lucy's rather colorful version of the events. Jane claims that there was absolutely nothing going on between her and Thomas at the time he left Lucy, that they got together considerably later. I have no doubt that Jane is telling the truth. But the fact that Lucy should volunteer an elaborate lie about what had finally tipped the scales, and particularly her clinging to the lie, make me think that knowing the real reason for Thomas's departure is perhaps the open sesame I need. It might give me a shot at understanding Lucy. Perhaps Thomas as well. Naturally, I asked Jane. She astonished me by saying that she didn't know; she was completely in the dark. Thomas didn't want to talk about it. She says that at this point only you and Lucy know what in fact happened. Will you tell me? It's certainly what Jane would like. As she put it, Lucy shouldn't be the only person filling in the blanks in Thomas's history. Or "brainwashing" me, to use your expression. You may well ask why it's any of my business to fill in the blanks. The answer is that the whole thing has become something of an obsession.

Let's order lunch, Alex replied. Will today's special be all right? Chopped steak and creamed spinach are first-rate here. You'll find yourself looking forward to them.

It was my turn to nod.

A glass of red house wine?

I nodded again.

I'm glad that's settled, he continued. And this obsession of yours: is it in reality the obsession with a book you want to write? Poor old Thomas is in no position to say yea or nay, but I can tell you that Miss De Bourgh will have your scalp if you stick her into a novel, and if I talk to you, and I'm still alive when your book appears, she'll go after mine too.

I gave Alex a variant of the answer I had given Lucy and said she'd been sufficiently reassured by it to go on speaking to me and in fact was eager to do so. Besides, I added, the book may never see the light of day. For instance, I might change my mind and want to work on something else, writing it may turn out to be too difficult, I could get sidetracked by another project.

One thing is clear, Alex said, if Lucy hasn't told you the real story in the first place she never will. I'm not sure how much good it will do you and your book to hear what happened, but it's a good story. I will not keep it from you if you give me your word that you'll never repeat it to anyone outside your book or breathe a word about having heard it from me. Especially to Miss Lucy.

I held out my hand and solemnly shook his.

All right, he said, there was no need to take what I say so literally. As I said, I'll take my chances on what you'll do in your book, but I don't want any chatter. I've got nothing scheduled for this afternoon. If you're free, we'll finish lunch and have coffee brought up to the card room. It's a good place to talk without being disturbed.

It's a story that goes way back, said Alex once our coffee had been served, and to tell it properly I have to go all the way back, not exactly to Adam and Eve but to Lucy and me. Some of this you've probably heard from Miss Lucy. If she has opened her kimono for you as wide as I infer, there were many opportunities to blast me, and I bet she hasn't missed a single one.

He paused and looked at me inquisitively. I nodded—sheepishly as I later realized—and said that she'd mentioned him once or twice.

That's what I figured, Alex said, laughing. The first thing, though, to keep in mind is that my parents, my sister, my brother, the nephews and nieces, and of course I all loved Thomas since he was a junior in high school and were all rooting for him when he got into Harvard and was offered the scholarship that made it possible for him to attend. The garage business wasn't then what it became, say, ten years later, when old Ben Snow made a bundle. Between you and me—I'm not sure that Lucy knows it—my father helped out a little too. Fast-forward to Thomas's senior year at college. To please Father, at the advanced age of thirty I condemned myself to the two-year course at the busy school. There I was, grinding away, and it occurred to me that for rest and recuperation, R and R is what we called it in the marines in my time, few activities could equal a roll in the hay with my old pal Lucy, with whom I'd been making sweet music—very discreetly—ever since she was in her last year at Miss Porter's. What a little hellion! She was in Bristol, you see, back from Paris, her heart broken by someone or other, at the time I had no idea who, her brother John told her I was in Cambridge, and she'd looked me up. Arranging to have her around was a dicey proposition because of Priscilla, whom I was seeing in New York and whom I'd decided I'd marry. I hadn't informed her of that plan but still . . . You say you remember Lucy from your Paris days as funny and, what else did you say, "devil-may-care"? Exactly right, but you should have known her at school and afterward at Radcliffe. Dynamite. Was the game worth the candle? I decided it was, and that is one gamble I've never regretted. I'd have her come down to a little apartment I'd taken in Boston and, my dear Philip, if those walls could speak! But all good things end. Once again between you and me, over Christmas Priscilla applied gentle pressure, I proposed, and my suit was accepted. My parents were thrilled, the Baldwin family being very much our kind of people. We've been together ever since, and that too is a gamble I've never regretted. But I had to tell Miss Lucy. She did not take the news well. Somehow she'd gotten the idea that she and I would tie the knot! Nothing could have been more foolish because, at the mere hint of such a match, Mother and Father would have gone up in smoke. Not because of the De Bourghs—who *entre nous* looked down their noses at the Baldwins—but because Lucy had acquired a certain reputation. It didn't help in managing the situation that Priscilla had never been able to stand her, not since school days, and that Lucy knew it. I succeeded in calming Lucy down, the R and R continued, my gratitude knew no bounds, and I began to consider seriously helping her relocate. That's when I thought of Thomas, who told me the last time I had seen him that a Radcliffe girl he'd been seeing had dumped him. I swung into action and gave a little cocktail party at my busy school digs to which I invited some of my more amusing classmates—rest assured that's not saying much—and the future lovebirds. I said nothing about my intentions to Thomas, but I explained to Lucy why he was, as she put it after she'd heard me out, a *bonne affaire*. To say that they hit it off is an understatement. I don't know whether they ended up in the sack that very evening, but the following week I offered them the use of my apartment in Boston. I wondered whether Lucy would be spooked by memories of her times there with me. I needn't have worried. She was a real trouper.

I've heard about the party from both of them, I murmured, scandalized by Alex's role as a full-service panderer and trying not to show it. But not about the apartment.

Alex laughed and said one or the other or both must have judged that detail too racy. The real question, one I've asked myself often, is what was I up to. So far as Lucy was concerned, the answer is relatively clear. I wanted her off my hands, with another interest to occupy her, and I knew that Thomas would be nice to her. But Thomas, did I think I was doing him a good turn? In retrospect, it wouldn't seem so, but at the time the outlook was different. I thought she'd civilize him—teach him better manners, show him how to dress, introduce him to a better sort of people—and give him lots of great sex. I suspected that his experience in that last department was sadly limited. I must say she did all that, just as I had imagined it, even the sex. Why else would he have become so besotted? Of course, it never occurred to me that there were any possible long-term consequences. Marriage— I would have said it was unthinkable. But as Henry Kissinger would have us believe, the unthinkable is always possible. I'll tell you what I believe really went wrong, why the marriage didn't work, perhaps couldn't work. It wasn't her being a little older or her having had too many rich and spicy experiences he didn't know about and probably wouldn't have understood or accepted or their coming from such wildly different backgrounds. All of that could have been accommodated, absorbed. No, the one thing I didn't take into account—and I don't understand how she could have failed to realize it and, if she did realize it, how she could have gone on to marry him—is that fundamentally she didn't like him. That's a problem that can't be fixed. Without simple affection, not sex but affection, a marriage can't work. Take Priscilla's and my marriage. We've had differences, I haven't been a model husband, but we genuinely like each other. We do the same things in order to be together. Nothing extraordinary that will surprise you. Our sailing days are over, I've sold the ketch, but we still play tennis, and Priscilla has even gotten me into a reading group. Not hers, of course, that's all ladies, but a sort of men's annex, so I can keep up!

Alex must have noticed the impatience I thought I had managed to repress and said, Hold on! Don't lose hope! We're almost at the end of the Ancient Testament presentation, with only one crucial fact to be added. It is my conviction that for all his intelligence and sensitivity either Thomas never figured out where Lucy and I stood when I introduced him to her, or if he had a glimpse of the truth he quickly buried it so deep that he never had to look at it again. The other side of the coin is that Lucy never told him, any more than she told him about the Swiss fellow.

I thought it best to raise my eyebrows and look puzzled.

Right, you haven't heard about him yet, he answered. You will. But to go back to what I was saying, I truly believe she never told him, however much she would have liked to stick the knife into him and into me. She realized that if she did there was a big risk that Thomas would be out the door. By the way, subsequent events prove I was right to think that would be his likely reaction if Hubert—that's the Swiss hero—ever surfaced. Certainly throwing Thomas out was something she daydreamed about. But putting herself in the wrong, and having him walk, that was not on the program. As a result, Thomas and I remained very close. If he didn't

think of me as an elder brother—he might have considered
that presumptuous—I was like a young uncle, someone who
understands you and whom you trust. You see what I mean.

I assured him I did, and that was the truth.

Thank you, he replied. Time out now for a pit stop. Do you
want to use the facilities?

I shook my head.

It's also time for a whiskey. Scotch and soda?

I said I'd love one.

All right, he said upon returning, the radiation I've had for
my little prostate trouble keeps me running to the loo. Ah,
here is the whiskey just when I need it. Fast-forward again,
to the year of the breakup. It was early May, a Tuesday. Priscilla and I had taken a long weekend in Newport, and I had
decided to skip coming here for lunch and to have a sandwich
at my desk instead. That was before we were bought by the
Germans, and Father was looking to me to keep us on an
even keel in some heavy headwinds. Just between you and
me, I've never worked so hard before or since. My secretary
had left for her lunch after bringing me mine, and I answered
the phone myself. It was Thomas. I could tell he was very
upset, and when he asked when he could see me I told him
to come right over. In my office he went straight to the point.
I'm going to tell you, he said, why I think I have to leave Lucy,
leave her today, and, yes, leave Jamie, and I want you to tell
me whether I'm insane. I said, Let's talk, but first I'll give you
a drink. I always kept some whiskey in my office and poured
him a stiff one. He drank it down and gave me an account
that was so coherent I think I remember it word for word.

I will repeat it for you now. Make believe that it's Thomas speaking, except when I interject a comment.

So here is what Thomas told me:

There is a man, he said, I've known since business school, he was my best friend there, Will Reading. You may have met him; he inherited the title while at the school and is now called Lord Reading. We also do a good deal of business together. He runs the family bank and happens to be in New York. We were going to have dinner tomorrow, with Lucy, but around ten this morning he called me and said he had to talk to me right away and suggested I come to his suite at the Carlyle.

"Remember when I called you from London soon after you and Lucy decided to get married," Will said practically as soon as I walked in, "and told you I'd come upon Lucy at the Savoy Grill having lunch with some fellow who said he was her cousin? She'd been holding hands with him and was none too pleased to see me. I called you because I thought I must. You decided to treat it as though it were nothing, and over the years I've thought that perhaps you were right. Lucy is quite a girl, and you've got Jamie." Reading was referring to a time right after our engagement when Lucy unexpectedly went to Paris, telling me that she had to make the trip in order to settle various things concerning her apartment and car. I was devastated by what Reading told me and wanted to break off the engagement. But Lucy swore up and down that it was nothing, that this fellow, a Swiss journalist, she said, with whom she was having lunch, was someone she had known years ago, and she had gone to London to let him know nicely and in person that she was getting married. I had a hard time believing her. We went over her story I don't know how many times, and in the end I decided to accept it as true. "By the way," Reading continued, "I have since met this fellow I called you about back then. I met him at a dinner in Geneva. His name is Hubert something or other, he is a very well-known journalist, and there is no question that he recognized me right away. My face must be fixed in his mind just as his is in mine. You remember that she told you that this fellow was working in London at the time of that lunch? That was pure twaddle. I made a discreet inquiry about his career, and he'd never been based there. More likely he and Lucy arranged to meet there. But that's not why I asked you to come here. Here is the reason. When I got back to the hotel yesterday afternoon, I'd say shortly after six, and was fiddling with the key trying to open the door to this suite, I heard French spoken behind me. Banal curiosity made me turn around, and what do you suppose I saw? In the door on the other side of the corridor stood Hubert kissing your own Lucy. She was barefoot, wearing one of those hotel peignoirs, and, I haven't a doubt, naked as a jay under it. Whether I made a noise, or they felt my presence for some other reason, he too turned around, so that he was no longer blocking her view, and all three of us stood there for a moment staring. The comic aspect got the better of me, and I said, Cheers, Lucy! I'm looking forward to dining with you and Thomas the day after tomorrow. Hubert is a big fellow and took a couple of steps in my direction. I thought he was going to slug me, but she screamed and, instead, he pushed her inside, went in himself, and slammed the door. I took a deep breath and went down to have a word with my friend the concierge and asked him whether Miss De Bourgh was staying at the hotel. Somehow I didn't think she'd use the name Snow. De Bourgh, he answered, of course Miss Lucy De Bourgh, she owns an apartment here. Ah yes, my lord, on your floor. You understand, the chap is a Brit. Used to be at Claridge's and knows me well. And Monsieur Brillard? His name had come back to me. Oh yes, my lord, he's here quite often. He is Miss De Bourgh's cousin and uses her apartment."

Alex, Thomas continued, I listened to Will, thinking I was locked inside a bad dream. But no, I was in my friend Reading's hotel suite, listening to his beautifully tuned voice, all those posh vowels, the slight stammer that doesn't interfere at all—indeed, makes him more eloquent—and he was offering me a scotch although it was before eleven. As I drank, the rich voice went on talking. "Thomas, old friend," it said, "I know I'm wounding you, but how could I keep this outrage from you?" You couldn't, I told him, you've done the right thing.

So that's the end of what Thomas told me that afternoon, Alex said. Now it's back to me, Alex.

What should I do? Thomas asked me, after he'd ended his story. Pretend I don't know? Let Reading come to dinner tomorrow—if he is willing to—and have him at most give Lucy a wink while I'm getting her another scotch? Or shall I leave her, which is what I want to do? If I leave, I think I have to leave today. I don't want to spend the night with her.

I told Thomas these were questions only he could answer.

However, I said that, if he chose to stay and pretend the conversation with Reading had not taken place, he might as well assume that Lucy would see through him. She'd know that he knew. Why would Reading decide not to tell you? I said. You're still close.

Yes, Thomas answered, and not just because of business. We see each other whenever he's here or I'm in London. And yes, I've put that same question to myself. She might think Reading decided not to say anything because that other time the warning he gave me had no effect except that it almost destroyed our friendship. I know that ever since he has felt awkward when Lucy is around. He could have said to himself, I won't interfere again, it can only get me in trouble.

That's possible, I said.

Thomas shook his head. It doesn't matter. I can't pretend I don't know. I can't live with her as though it hadn't happened. And I wouldn't be able to believe her if we had it out and she promised never to do it again. Really, it comes down to Jamie. How can I leave him with her? How can I live without him?

This is when I asked Thomas: Will you be really leaving him? Won't he be leaving you, going away to school? Don't you think that she'll agree to some reasonable arrangement about visits and that sort of thing?

Thomas said that if he could be objective about the situation he'd reason just as I had: Jamie was graduating from Buckley; a young master from St. Bernard's who'd been a combination tutor and babysitter, taking him after school for the last three years, had agreed to be with him this summer in

Little Compton, since Lucy had declared she'd only be there for three weeks in August and he wasn't sure of being able to take all of July; and, indeed, starting in the fall, Jamie would be at Exeter. And then he asked me whether I thought he could—or should—simply go to the apartment after he'd left me, pack his stuff, say goodbye to Jamie, and go to a hotel. He'd thought of the Harvard Club or the Paddock, but he didn't want to be where he'd run into people he knew.

I told him he was in for a bad time, but he had better get on with it. Then, as I was imagining what the scene over there at their apartment would be like, it occurred to me that he shouldn't be alone that evening, and I asked him to have dinner with us. Drinks at the apartment, we'll go somewhere or other afterward. Can you imagine it? Thomas got very emotional, and he said he would like that, that he had always known he could count on me to protect him. This is how I got the story of what happened when he went home that very evening.

Lucy was there, Thomas told Priscilla and me, as were Jamie and the St. Bernard's fellow, his name has just come back to me, Hugh Cowles, *entre nous* someone we'd met any number of times, good family and all that, who has the looks and manner of a fairy but in fact is a rather active ladies' man who'd been briefly married to one of the Phipps girls. Lucy put down the receiver—she'd been on the telephone in the library when Thomas arrived—and said, My my, you're home early, or something like that. Are you sick? He didn't reply, got his bag out of a hall closet, and went into the bedroom to pack. But he found he really couldn't. He was in a coffin made of glass, dead although perfectly conscious and capable of speech, and conscious of the pointlessness of every action. Nevertheless, he threw in the suitcase his toilet kit, with sleeping pills in it, a couple of shirts and pairs of underpants and socks, and one suit. He added the photographs of Jamie from the dresser. All the while Lucy was screaming, Don't do it, Thomas, you're making a dreadful mistake, what that bastard Reading told you is nothing, it will never happen again, and he could hear and understand what she was saying but couldn't answer. She was far away and he in his coffin. Still in the coffin, he went to Jamie's room, waited until Cowles had left, told Jamie, and tried to comfort him. The kid cried and cried. And still in his coffin, he pushed Lucy aside when she tried to block the front door. I really wanted to hit her, he said, and not just once, but I didn't. So he got into the elevator, had the doorman hail a taxi, and drove to the Hilton on Sixth Avenue.

What a ghastly business, I said.

Alex nodded. Awful. One moment of comedy: when Thomas told me that evening as we were having drinks that he was down to two suits, the one he was wearing and the one waiting in the hotel, I said that was all for the best. It was time he stopped wearing those Brooks Brothers standard-issue numbers and let my tailor make him some grown-up clothes. But that will never do, he replied, Lucy has always said I'm not white enough for Anderson and Sheppard and never will be.

Alex and I had another whiskey and left the club together. It was the hour when taxi drivers turn on the OFF DUTY sign

and head for meeting places somewhere near the Queens-
boro Bridge and switch with drivers working the next shift.
It's hopeless, said Alex, I'll toddle off. I asked whether he
still lived at the River House. Indeed, he told me, whereupon
I offered to walk him home. It took us longer than I had
expected. The arthritis in his right knee was getting worse,
and he leaned heavily on his cane. He planned to have the
knee replaced after the summer. Priscilla and I play tennis all
winter, he told me. I'll be rushing the net again in no time.

As we were parting he asked me: Do you understand them
better?

Not yet, I told him.

Well, said Alex, let me add to your confusion. A month
or so after that day of drama, when Thomas already had an
apartment and had moved into it, we had lunch at the club.
We chatted about Jamie and the difficult time he was going
through and how he, Thomas, in his mind had been going
over and over the breakup and the chronology of his awful
marriage. I was commiserating with him, conscious, I must
say, of the role I had played in that affair, when all of a sudden
Thomas said, Stop, Alex! I'm going to tell you something that
may make you think I'm crazy. If I had my life to live again,
there is still no way I could stop myself from marrying her.

X

THERE WAS TO BE no immediate attempt on my part to find an answer to the question Alex had asked while we were saying goodbye. No, I wasn't sure I understood Thomas and Lucy better, and I wasn't sure that I cared. A great impatience had overcome me. The moment I got home, without even checking telephone messages, I sat down at my desk and started work on the real book, stored in my laptop, that was nearing completion, and banished all thoughts of Lucy and Thomas. Their book, I had told myself as I walked west and then uptown after I had dropped off Alex, was a pipe dream; and in comparison with the crisis faced by the characters I had invented, the travails of Lucy and Thomas, however real, were unconvincing, perhaps even lacking in authenticity! Had Tolstoy ever said that all unhappy marriages are alike? If he hadn't, he should have: I felt I had stumbled on an important truth. Whether or not I had, I worked hard that afternoon and early evening, didn't allow my mind to wander, and by nine o'clock I had overshot my daily target of twelve hundred words. Tired and drained of ideas, I had a bath, put on a CD of Haydn sonatas, a recent present from a German friend, and made myself a dinner of scrambled eggs, soft Vermont goat cheese, two peaches—the first ripe ones I had been able to find at the supermarket—and a half bottle of Côtes du Rhône. I ate at the kitchen table. In the state of relaxation induced by the music and the wine, I surrendered guiltily to my fixation on Lucy and Thomas.

Alex had told me that the last time he saw Thomas was toward the end of January 1998, less than two weeks before the accident in Bahia. That put it less than a year after my own last meeting with Thomas and Jane, in Paris, in mid-April 1997. Thomas claimed that the Supreme Court had made a fatal mistake by ruling that Paula Jones could pursue her sexual harassment lawsuit against President Clinton while he was still in office. They've opened a true Pandora's box, he said, and put the country on the road to a wholly unnecessary constitutional crisis.

Jane found Thomas's position unprincipled and shocking. If there is anything to the story that woman has told under oath, why should he get away with that sort of behavior just because soon after it took place he was elected president?

No reason, he answered, except that there will be no end to the way he will be harassed. Don't forget that this fellow Kenneth Starr has all the right wing nuts in the country egging him on. He'll put every piece of Clinton's dirty laundry on public view, all of his mostly revolting sexual peccadilloes, and do serious damage to his presidency. It's all right with the American public if the president wastes his time on the golf links. But sex! They'll crucify him for it, even though it's a pastime that takes less time and is probably better for you than golf.

The service at the restaurant on avenue Montaigne to which Thomas had invited me because of a review Jane had read praising the genius of its celebrity chef was desperately slow. It being a Tuesday, when French museums were closed, Thomas had arranged for them a private visit of the royal apartments in Versailles. They were running late, and our meal ended in slight disarray, with promises to get back together before they left Paris but no concrete plan. On the way back to my apartment, walking first along Cours Albert Ier and then the quays, I wished I had eaten less and renewed my vow to avoid gastronomic lunches with visiting Americans, even those I liked a lot. In fact, we didn't see one another again during that visit. I would have normally looked them up when I came to the States for the summer, but I flew nonstop to the West Coast, where I taught a class in a creative writing program at Berkeley, and from there I went directly to Sharon. I called when I finally passed through New York on my way back to Paris, but they were out of town. That missed opportunity was the last one; when I next traveled to New York, he had been dead for months. The obituary ran in the *Herald Tribune* as well as the *New York Times,* and there were substantial articles in the *Wall Street Journal* and the *Economist.* All of them included a vivid description of the accident. Thomas had been swimming off a Bahia beach and was killed by a speedboat with a water skier in tow. The driver, alone in the boat, had been steering with one hand, his head turned in the direction of the skier, whom he didn't want to lose from sight. Both the boat and the skier ran over Thomas, the boat most likely killing him at once, while Jane, who had waded deep into the water as the scene unfolded, wailed and wailed.

These random memories, as in truth everything I recalled about Thomas, were vivid, but it occurred to me that because of the fascination Lucy held for me, and perhaps also because I remembered Thomas so well that I could, in a sense, take him for granted, I had been focusing almost exclusively on her. I had liked him and had enjoyed his company; that seemed to wrap it up. But it was becoming clear that if I was going to understand what had happened to him and Lucy as a couple, I had better try to think about him more analytically. Whether I was up to it I couldn't tell, for reasons not unrelated to how I read and write. For example, I've never thought I knew what a novel—somebody else's or mine—is "about," a failing that has made it difficult to earn a modest supplementary income as an occasional book reviewer or to answer journalists wanting to know what message readers should take away from my most recent book. My stock reply to that last question—one that is in fact quite sincere and not a lame attempt to coin a koan—is that a book is about what it says. Similarly, my characters are the sum of their actions and words as reported by me, so that a string of defining epithets—handsome, intelligent, ambitious, courteous, shy—doesn't add much that a reader would find valuable. If a further gloss of that sort were required, I doubted that I could do better than something on the order of "godlike Thomas, beloved of Hermes and swift to climb."

For the truth was that Thomas had climbed with rare skill, and few people could bear witness to his ascent more authoritatively than I, who had invited the polite and garrulous GI on leave to what must have been his first Parisian cocktail party and, some forty years later, was his guest at the hottest restaurant in Paris and saw him offer to Jane, whom a gossip columnist might have termed, however unjustly, a trophy wife, golden apples from the highest branch of the tree of success. I am not thinking only of the suite at the Ritz, the black BMW driven by a chauffeur in uniform that had brought them from the hotel to the restaurant, and into which they climbed en route to a palace normally overrun by tourists and schoolchildren that they would visit in peace and quiet accompanied only by a senior curator. Those were perquisites of a very rich man, of whom there are so many, and Thomas had indeed become very rich. I supposed he had made handsome gifts toward the restoration of the château, perhaps he was on the board of the American association that had done so much for Versailles. It was also possible that in his case it was sufficient to be who he was. But the day before, he and Jane had lunched at the Élysée Palace with the president, who wanted to quiz Thomas about the root causes of the Mexican debt crisis of the 1980s and the restructuring that followed and more generally the lessons it held for banks lending to Russia. And two days later, Jane and he were having dinner with the head of the Banque de France, someone

Thomas had gotten to know well who was interested in some of the same issues. It was clear, and indeed it had been clear to me for a long time, that through unusual gifts and force of personality Thomas had risen to a sphere that was frequented by only the rarest of financiers and that he had ascended as a self-made man. I thought of his occasional accounts of the crisis that had engulfed first Mexico and then one country south of the border after another, the conclusions he had drawn, and the process of making his ideas sufficiently acceptable to government officials who were his clients for them to take the actions he thought necessary. They were intellectual and dispassionate, and very unlike the war stories told by other high-level investment bankers—for instance, my cousin Josiah—those heroic boasts about huge deals whose fate had hung on a thread before they were rescued by a telephone call they had made in the dead of the night. Once in a while I had heard Thomas as well speak about the human aspect of his business exploits, but the hallmark of his anecdotes was invariably wistful self-deprecation.

Why then have I allowed myself to think that Thomas had "climbed," with all the denigrating implications of that expression? Where were my egalitarian, left-of-center ACLU biases and pretensions? The finger pointed at the unreconstructed snob inside me, who could not take his eyes off a damning piece of evidence: barely hatched, the self-made man had had the temerity to marry a highborn heiress. These sour thoughts took me back to the afternoon when Lucy first brought him to my apartment and my amusement at her having a beau who was of all things a townie! And, as I pondered my offhand response, I had to conclude that my choice of the odious verb had been spot on: of course, Thomas had climbed, and Lucy wasn't wrong to rail that he had wanted to arrive and had used her as a stepladder. He had taken advantage of her social position and her modest fortune, which at the time must have seemed to him pretty grand. But how could it have been otherwise if they were to marry, or even—inconceivable at the time—simply live together in sin? Could he have avoided meeting her family and friends? Would she have liked to spend her and Thomas's summer vacations and Christmas, Thanksgiving, and other holidays with Mrs. and Mrs. Snow Sr. in their aluminum-shingle colonial somewhere on the wrong side of the tracks in Newport, in preference to the manse she had inherited in Little Compton or the De Bourgh family seat in Bristol? Would she have wanted to live within his means during the period of however many years when he was still a student or when his salary was a pittance? That would have meant residing in Waltham or Somerville rather than on Beacon Street while he was still at the business school and later when she was continuing with her treatment and he had the business-school research and teaching assignment, and in Brooklyn or in the wilds of the West Side, or, horror of horrors, Hoboken, once they had moved to New York. Would that have suited her? If my memory of my first visit to them on Park Avenue was correct, the answer was no. She would have had to do without nannies, full-time cleaning ladies, and housekeepers; one cannot imagine how she would have coped with Jamie. The other side of the coin is that if she had been a long-term investor or even a gambler with steady nerves, if she had been careful to hang on to Thomas instead of goading him into a divorce by a stunt that was truly beyond the pale, in material terms she would have done quite well. He would have most likely stuck with her, and she would have inevitably had her turn at the racetrack betting window, collecting the rich payout. She would have ended up "using" Thomas, his position and his money. Could a couple stay together if one partner begrudged the other what had been given or received unequally? I didn't think so, and if I was right, the real question might be whether, in a couple that wasn't in approximate equilibrium, "climbing" had been the purpose of the partner who was poorer or socially inferior at the outset. It was a bet I couldn't win or lose, but I would have wagered any amount that Thomas had married Lucy because he had fallen for her and hadn't wanted to lose her, which he feared he would if he didn't take the plunge. That is not to deny, however, that tucked inside him was a strong instinct for self-preservation, that he would not have risked marrying a woman with her lifestyle, to use an odious expression that was not yet in use at the time, her assumptions about what life owed her, and her psychological fragility, if she had not had enough money. And because Thomas wasn't quite the straight arrow he sometimes seemed, who could say whether Lucy's lifestyle and fragility had not been the catnip he couldn't resist, a fragrance as powerful as the sex?

Having reread my words, I had to laugh at the notion of catnip. If the sweet smell of Lucy's money and Social Register connections had determined Thomas, or had given him an ever so slight push over the line, he'd been a fool. Certainly, Lucy's money had made life in Boston and in New York much more comfortable in the early years. Certainly, he had been able to savor guiltily and mostly in secret the sweetness of the De Bourghs' historical importance and social position, condiments that had also heightened the pleasure of screwing Miss Lucy. But the leg up she had given him, the footstool she'd been? Pure bunk! In its place I saw the contempt in which she'd held him, and how it and the discord between her and Thomas had sapped his energy and, had he been less resilient, would not have failed to clip his wings. There was no getting around it. It wasn't just Lucy: they had both made a hash of it.

Inexorably, I was led back to Alex's diagnosis, that the marriage had been doomed because, when you came right down to it, Lucy didn't like Thomas. Alex was probably right. If she had liked him, she would have been more generous, and Hubert would not have been allowed to come back into her life. But why hadn't she liked him? He was good-looking, pleasant, and manifestly destined to succeed. She had picked him. Where had she gone wrong?

In the morning, I set out for Zabar's with the intention of stocking up on smoked fish I would take with me to Sharon the next day, when I moved there for the summer. On Broadway, when I was no more than a hundred yards away from the store, a young woman a few steps ahead of me, talking with great animation into her cell phone, veered toward the curb in order to claim the cab that was discharging a passenger. Unaware, perhaps because my eyes were fixed on her huge head of curly red hair, of the small suitcase she was pulling behind her, I kept walking without changing direction myself until I tripped on something that turned out to be the leash attached to the suitcase. My hands had been clasped behind my back—a habit that is half affectation and half an attempt to alleviate the permanent pain in my lower back. I did not bring them forward fast enough to cushion the fall, and I heard an impressive thud when my forehead hit the sidewalk. The young woman said, Gee, I'm sorry, and got into the cab. Two or three people stopped to observe me. Anxious not to require their assistance or sympathy, I got up smartly, dusted off my trousers and canvas-duck jacket, and was ready to continue to Zabar's, when one of the bystanders raised her hand and told me I had better do something about the bleeding. I touched my forehead and brought back fingers covered with blood. Next I looked at myself in a store window and saw that the bigger source of the bleeding was a gash in my right eyebrow. There was also a less-alarming abrasion directly above it.

Sewing up my cuts at the St. Luke's–Roosevelt Hospital emergency room, just beyond Lincoln Center, took less time than I had feared, and I was relieved to learn that the doctor in Sharon would be able to remove the stitches. No change in my schedule was required. I had a sandwich and a big latte at Le Pain Quotidien on West Sixty-Fifth Street and, pleased with my newly displayed stoicism, got my errands done at Zabar's, packed as soon as I got home, wrote notes to people who I thought might be interested, however tepidly, in my departure, and, after another dinner of scrambled eggs, cheese, peaches, and wine, went to bed. The painkiller the emergency room doctors had given me had the desired hypnotic effect. The dreams I was convinced it had also procured were so swinish that I was able to disregard them. I got up in the morning refreshed, admired my patched-up face in the bathroom mirror, got the car out of the garage, loaded my meager possessions, and drove to Sharon, *procul negotiis,* as far from the affairs of men as I could manage.

In the third week of August I received a telephone call from Bill Taylor. He was at his house in Lenox; the Tanglewood festival crowds had driven him bats. Was I working too hard to contemplate having a guest, even one who was not only self-sufficient but asked for nothing better than to be allowed to scribble all day, and did I have room? Having finished a complete first draft of my new novel, I was giving myself a breather before starting the serious rereading of the text and the revisions that would follow. But even if I had been in the midst of composition, even if I had been on deadline—a condition I had now managed to avoid for many years—I would have told Bill the same truth: that I was jumping up and down for joy at the prospect of seeing him and that he must come as soon as possible and stay until he was good and tired of Sharon. There is always a little selfish idea in the back of a writer's head. Mine was that I might get my text printed out in the village, a practice that cost money but avoided putting too much strain on my aged printer, and get Bill to read it. He was a few years older than I; like Alex he had been in the war, and I believe had been in Alex's class at college. Unlike him, however, Bill had had nothing to do with the *Lampoon,* final clubs, or even the Signet. His father refused to give him a dime, and he had had no money beyond his scholarship, the GI Bill, and however much of his army pay he had been able to save. Archie MacLeish had admitted him to his writing class in the fall of his freshman year, an unusual if not unprecedented distinction. A collection of Bill's short stories was published some months after his graduation. I had recognized the quality of his talent as soon as I read them, and my admiration for his work kept growing with the appearance of each new book, of which there were now many.

We didn't meet until I went to live in Paris, probably because he hadn't participated in the sillier aspects of undergraduate life. By then he had become close to a number of people involved with the *Paris Review,* one or two of whom I knew well. But the introduction was made by my friend Guy Seurat, who had become his French publisher—as well as Bella's and mine. Bill was from New Orleans, where for generations his family had run a livery business that eventually evolved into a carting and moving company. The South was a world I knew only from the southern school of writers, which was then in great vogue. Bill's works were markedly different from theirs. Mordant and cerebral, shunning flights of rhetoric, his tales of siblings' internecine struggles over property were closer in mood and outlook to Mauriac's depictions of cannibalism as practiced by the bourgeoisie of the Bordeaux region than to the treatment of not dissimilar themes by Faulkner and, later, Flannery O'Connor. Like many American writers and artists, he drifted away from Paris in the sixties—I had remained because of Bella—found he didn't like the way oil and gas money was transforming New Orleans, came back to Paris frequently, staying in a pied-à-terre in the Marais, but in the seventies and the eighties had lived principally in a fourth-floor railroad walk-up on upper Lexington Avenue that he shared with Dick Berger, a conceptual artist slowly becoming fashionable. Toward the end of that period, after Dick had dumped him unceremoniously, Bill bought an old house on a quiet side street in Lenox. We had hit it off in Paris, becoming good professional colleagues. But it was Bella whom Bill had loved, who knew the ins and outs of his affairs, including the disastrous entanglement with Dick, and who dispensed advice and consolation. Once we had fixed up the house in Sharon, Bill started a tradition of visiting us there each summer, usually around Labor Day. He drew closer to me after she died, as though I had been left to him in her will. He too was alone now; one younger man after another left him for reasons Bill couldn't fathom or didn't care to discuss.

A couple of days after his arrival I invited my cousin Josiah and his wife, Molly, to dinner. Bill liked them. Our meals with them, and whichever of their daughters and granddaughters happened to be around, had also become a tradition. This time they came alone. We ate on the screened porch seated so that we could all admire the moon, which had risen early

and hung over us like a yellow lantern. I had dispensed with
the services of Mrs. James and served steaks I broiled on my
small outdoor grill, boiled new potatoes, and a tomato salad,
followed by a peach tart baked by Mrs. James's daughter. It
was the kind of dinner Bella would have chosen for a hot
August night, and I couldn't help being pleased that I had
pulled it off. Except for Molly, who was going to drive, we
drank more of my old Chinon than was reasonable, and I
didn't mind Josiah's ribbing me about my conferences with
Alex and general obsession with Thomas and Lucy.

Really, Bill interjected, Philip still sees her? I kicked the
habit so long ago that if you asked me whether she was dead
or alive I would have had to say I'm not sure. I do know that
Thomas died some years ago, and she certainly wasn't dead
at the time of the accident. The *Times* said he'd been survived
by both wives. Of course, I know Jane. She's interviewed me.
I confess that I used to know Lucy very much better; we'd see
each other all the time in Paris and then in New York, when
Dick Berger and I were still together. I even knew Thomas;
I'd see him in New York. Then it was all over. Still, why do
you suppose the thought that Lucy might not be alive has
crossed my mind? Wishful thinking?

Josiah laughed. It's because dying has become such a habit!
But rest assured. Lucy's alive and kicking. Philip can fill you
in. He is currently the world's leading expert.

I hadn't liked the bitchy edge of Bill's remarks about Lucy
and was glad that the conversation veered to Iraq. The day
before, a suicide bomber had blown up the UN headquarters in Baghdad killing the UN's head representative in

Iraq and more than a dozen other people. The cluelessness of Paul Bremer, our new proconsul, the incipient religious war in that benighted country, the looting of its art treasures that our military failed to stop, and the sneak attacks on our troops filled all of us with apprehension and gloom. At least we've gotten rid of Saddam, Josiah interjected, breaking the silence. Bill protested that if America was on a quest to slay dragons, there were many others waiting in line, some even more monstrous, like Kim Jong Il. He for one was convinced that if we continued on that path the end result would be the demoralization of our country and the eventual unhinging of its economy. All his money, he said, except for an amount in cash that he figured was roughly equal to one year's expenses, was in stocks. Should he sell? If he sold, what should he buy? Josiah gave him long-winded advice about the need to diversify and the virtues of investing in equities. As for himself, he said he was buying gold for his family's life-buoy fund. Gold coins. You could always find a buyer, even if some crisis made you unable to get your money from the ATM. In addition, unless you're dumb, you'll be able to finesse paying tax on the gain. And believe me, he added, if you hold gold you will have gains.

The next day I screwed up my courage and asked Bill whether he would read the draft. He said he'd be glad to. In return, he wanted to know about my new interest in Lucy.

I noticed, he added, that I shocked you by what I said about her yesterday evening. I'd had one bourbon too many before dinner and too much of your wine. The fact is I can't forgive her for how she behaved when Dick and I broke up. Perhaps I should, but I can't.

I told him my interest was anything but new; I too had known her in Paris, had seen her on and off in New York, and in May, right after my return to New York, I'd run into her at the ballet. The change in her had shocked and fascinated me. I didn't mean the change in her appearance—in that respect she was doing as well as could be hoped. It was the simmering anger that could at any moment, one felt, boil over as rage, resentment, and bitterness the potential for which I had not detected in her before. She'd become humorless. The rawness of her hostility toward Thomas, perhaps hatred, even though the guy had been dead since 1998, and they'd been divorced for at least twenty-five years, shocked and surprised me. What had he done to her? What had she done to him? As I said, the guy is dead, and while he was alive he wasn't all that bad. I had liked him.

Bill laughed and said, It's not all that mysterious. She's fucked up her life. Deep down she knows it, but that's no help because she can't and won't admit she's done it to herself and so must find someone else to blame. Thomas has been the logical candidate, and now the poor guy can't even try to defend himself. I really did know her very well, both in Paris and in New York. In fact, I was her bosom friend and father confessor, though not her director of conscience, and did she ever need one! That stopped when Dick left me and she took his side—gratuitously, stupidly, and viciously. As I told you, I've not forgiven her; we haven't communicated since then. Not that she has tried to apologize or make up! No, admitting that she's in the wrong isn't in her DNA. Anyway, to go back to the time when we were best friends, a sort of relationship that develops more often than you probably realize between a gay man and a girl who gets herself banged by practically everyone she meets, including weirdos like that Swiss guy Hubert. She must have someone to talk to. Who could be more comfy than a nice queer like me who happens to like the company of women? She could tease my cock all she wanted, without having to put out, and get sympathy from someone whose own sex life wasn't then and isn't now all that simple. I used to tell her my troubles too! Did you know the dreaded Hubert? Come to think of it, you must. He was friends with Guy Seurat.

I shook my head and added that I'd heard about him—from Lucy.

Just as well you didn't have the pleasure, said Bill, he was a nasty piece of work. The key to Lucy is that she's a goddamn romantic. She's probably told you that Hubert fucked like a god, or something like that, and that he was at the time an important journalist. I think, though, what clinched the deal was his status as a fearless and very competent mountain climber. That's on top of the skiing. Do you know about that?

Again, I shook my head.

Well, he's climbed the north face of the Matterhorn alone, with just one guide, and also the north face of the Eiger, which is said to be a real killer. If he hadn't existed, she'd have had to invent him: a sadist with a big death wish! What more could Lucy have wanted? Or take the fling she had with Aly Khan! Do you know about that? He tucked her in between Rita Hayworth and Bettina. They'd go on those wild nighttime dashes to Deauville because one of his horses was doing something or other and he had to be there. She told me afterward that she's never been so scared in her life as with him in one of his cars. The sex, as described by her, was life threatening too.

I didn't know about Aly, I said. I guess I didn't read the right papers.

They managed to keep it very quiet, Bill replied. I don't know how they did it, but it worked, the only squib in the press was in *Paris-presse*: Prince Aly adds American aristocrat to his *haras,* his stud farm. No other paper picked it up.

The recollection made Bill laugh so hard tears came into his eyes. He wiped them and continued. I'll propound a theory worthy of Havelock Ellis. For neurotic romantics like Lucy, real sexual attraction, and what you might call love, exist at two antipodes. One is inhabited by generic romantic lovers, preferably artists or writers. These are the good guys, but they're not allowed to be weak, which when you think of most of our colleagues is a big problem. Domineering bastards and sadists are on the prowl at the other antipode. That's Hubert's domain. The question is how did Miss Lucy with her De Bourgh pride and so forth—someone in Paris who knew the parents well, perhaps the ambassador with whom I was quite chummy, once told me De Bourghs didn't believe they piss and shit like other people—justify to herself letting him use her the way he did once the heavy stuff began? That's where I believe and I'd bet anything the aura of adventure—his skiing, Matterhorn and Eiger—were useful credentials. They validated what she was doing—and even more important what he was doing to her. That leaves the space between the antipodes, where only casual sex can and does take place. It is there, in that empty lot, I am convinced, that she met Thomas, and that is where the affair with him should have remained. We don't know whether Lucy in fact has ever had the ideal romantic lover, or who he might have been, but he sure wasn't Thomas. And Thomas, unfortunately for him, wasn't Hubert lite either. If only! Then she would have loved him madly and forgiven him everything unless, like Hubert, he really crossed a bright red line. But as it was, poor Thomas was fated to have a raw deal.

I should tell you, he continued, that I had many occasions to observe the Snow ménage in action. Dick and I got the place on Lexington Avenue soon after they settled in the city. She and I had been in touch, so we got together right away. It was pathetic how she was gasping for breath, desperate not to be smothered by the boredom of the existence those two had staggered into: those office colleagues with whom Thomas wanted her to socialize, other bankers, Josiah included, lawyers with whom he worked on deals. What a distance from the sort of people to whom she'd gotten accustomed in Paris! Actually, many of the Paris crowd were here, but she had lost track of them, and they hadn't been exactly looking for her. Between you, me, and the doorpost, so far as most were concerned she'd been nothing more than a hanger-on who gave little cocktail parties and dinners with good food. That had been useful to them in Paris, but even if she'd tried to lure them in New York, it cut no ice. You know how such things go. Old friends drop into a black hole or become too successful. So I did my best. For instance, I got her together with Penny Stone, you probably remember her, a southern girl who'd been studying painting, did some modeling, and turned to photography and was doing shoots for *Vogue*. She took Lucy to gallery openings and introduced her to some of her friends. There was Mac Howell, a pretty good poet. Through him she met Gianfranco Rossi and a whole gang of painters. Of course none of them was respectable from Thomas's point of view, some of them, especially Mac, drank a lot, and they smoked pot—or hash if they could get it—and some dropped LSD. Hell, we all did, and Lucy quite liked the pot and the hash! She didn't have the nerve to try any of the really good stuff. Anyway, in Thomas's opinion they weren't people who could be invited to dinner or whatever with his friends. Then Dick and I began to have an open house party on Thursday evenings. Let me tell you, everyone came. It would get so jam-packed that people were queuing in the staircase. Of course, I issued a standing invitation to Lucy and Thomas. She came regularly, and for a while Thomas came too because he'd recognized that these were happenings, social events that were mentioned in gossip columns and so forth. Lucy did just fine in that setting, just as she had in Paris, but Thomas had a way of creating a void around himself. He wasn't rude—just icy and covertly hostile. You didn't have to have a particularly thin skin to sense that he was uncomfortable, that he wished he were somewhere else, that he certainly would have preferred to be talking to someone else, and, above all, that he disapproved. They must have had it out about how he antagonized people at our parties, because after a while she always came alone. He plain stopped showing up. So Lucy went on meeting Penny and Mac and some of the others in bars or at Penny's, and they drank and got stoned together, but the idea of her creating the kind of salon she more or less had in Paris was out of the question. Not with the aptly named boreal Thomas Snow! There is a whole other chapter to be written, by the way. At a time when we all, Lucy included, locked elbows and demonstrated against the war, Thomas was for LBJ. He thought he was a great president! He thought we were in Vietnam to protect our vital interests. Of course, he recanted long before the Pentagon Papers came out, but all the same he remained in deep disgrace.

You really disliked him, I ventured. Lucy married Charles Bovary! Is that what you're telling me? Why not come out and say it?

Not at all, Bill answered, although one learns a great deal more from novels than from life. I liked him all right, and of all the Paris hands he met in New York during that time I was the only one he seemed to take to and approve of. Not exclusively because of my charm, I believe. My modest celebrity played a role. His friends would have read reviews, some even knew my books, so I was a quasi bohemian who could be invited with them. No, there was nothing wrong with Thomas if you took him on his terms, as a very bright, very ambitious, bound-to-succeed, nice-looking investment banker, with very good manners that had been learned. I do not think they came from the heart. Charles Bovary? Certainly not. Thomas wasn't a stupid oaf; he was self-aware, and I'd bet dollars to doughnuts that nothing I have told you about the effect he'd had on Lucy's friends would have come to him as a surprise. He most certainly didn't botch any operations on anyone's clubfoot. Metaphorically speaking, of course. In fact, to my knowledge the only really stupid thing he ever did was to marry Miss De Bourgh.

Had Bill deepened my understanding of Lucy? I thought he probably had, making me visualize an aspect of her life with Thomas I knew nothing about. He was right not to see Thomas as a sort of Charles Bovary—of that I was sure—and Lucy, with her intelligence, haughty sense of caste, and, let's face it, money, was worlds away from the beautiful provincial fool who had read too many novels. But I had not made much progress in my effort to see Thomas more clearly. Except for one thought that was taking form in my mind: that there was no mystery; he was quite simply what he appeared to be, a fine example of the American dream come true. Work hard and succeed! And he had had all the necessary equipment: high intelligence and good looks. There was also the fact that he had managed to make a beautiful and devilishly bright girl like Jane happy. Not a bad reference, Jane's having appar-

LOUIS BEGLEY

ently been happy with her lawyer husband Horace until he had crossed her red line, and being by her own admission happy with her current banker husband, Ned, didn't lessen its relevance or weight. Putting Horace's peccadilloes aside, all three corresponded to a type she found acceptable. Jane was no romantic; she was a modern American woman perfectly clear about what she wanted.

XI

FEW DAYS AFTER Bill left for Lenox, a FedEx
envelope addressed to me arrived at my house in
Sharon, an unusual event unless I am working on
a manuscript with the rare editor who isn't too cheap to use
that service. Inside the envelope I found, to my considerable surprise, a long letter from Jamie. He wrote that he
had intended to visit me in New York and then, after he
had learned from Jane that I had moved to the country for
the balance of the summer, had decided to ask to see me in
Sharon, that his plans for travel to the East Coast had been
frustrated by Stella's—that was his wife's name—pregnancy.
Having had two successive miscarriages late in term, she
was understandably nervous about his being away. The baby
wasn't due until November; doubtless it would be difficult
to leave right after it had been born, and he didn't want to
postpone getting in touch with me until the New Year. There
followed a development, which I found very touching, about

old memories: the occasional weekend foray with his father and me to P.J. Clarke's and the cheeseburgers that still made his mouth water, the Tintin and Astérix comic books I used to bring him from Paris, the time his father and he spent a week with Aunt Bella—an appellation that invariably brings tears to my eyes—and me at the house we owned at the time on Île de Ré, and the fun it had been to go out in my sailboat. He hoped I would allow him to show me some of his recent work, including the adaptation he had completed of a Jack London novel, which actually seemed likely to go into production.

Then he came to the point. He'd heard from Jane that I'd been talking to her and Lucy about his father and, just like everybody connected with Lucy and his father's "case," he wanted his testimony to be entered on the record. Some of what he wrote I had already heard. The firsthand account of the effect of the breakup on Jamie was new and saddened me deeply:

Dad stormed out and Mom went absolutely bonkers. She made herself a drink, put on her favorite 45 rpm with this Piaf song "Rien de rien, non je ne regrette rien de rien" and played it over and over and over. She danced to it, drink in hand. Then it was suddenly summer, and it was surely the worst summer of my life. Mom and Dad hadn't worked out anything before he left, such things as when I could see him, what would happen during vacations, and other stuff of that sort, and they were really furious at each other, totally unable to communicate. Right after graduation, Mr. Cowles, the St. Bernard's master who tutored me, and I went up to Little Compton. Mrs. Smith, the cook, went with us to keep house. Mom said she had to stay in the city until her doctor went on vacation, but she drove up on weekends, green about the gills and as cross as two sticks. Those weekends weren't great. Mr. Cowles would take off, as did the cook, and I had to tiptoe around the house because Mom mostly slept. Or she'd go out and leave Mrs. Ticknor, an old biddy with bad breath, in charge because she thought it was wrong not to have an adult in the house. Not that I needed her, at the age of fourteen, in a very safe community. Anyway, although Mom didn't know it, Mrs. Ticknor would start hitting the liquor closet pretty hard as soon as Mom was out of the driveway. She'd been Mom's social science teacher or something; Mom explained to Mr. Cowles and me that the Ticknors were a very good Rhode Island or Connecticut family that had lost all its money. Mr. Cowles—I was actually calling him Hugh by that time—was really into that sort of thing. Finally, I turned Mrs. T. in to Mom. You can imagine the row. Afterward, Mrs. Ticknor came by the house when Mom had gone back to the city and cursed me and said she was giving me the evil eye! During the week it was actually all right, because Hugh and I would go to the club to play tennis in the morning, and in the afternoon we'd sail the Mercury Dad had given me for graduation. Then came the real big row, when Dad arrived on a Tuesday and took me to Newport because it was my grandfather Snow's seventieth birthday. We came back pretty early in the evening, but in the meantime Mom had called and asked to speak to me, and Hugh had no choice: he told her where I was. Mom went wild and yelled at him, then yelled at me when we got back, and when Dad took the telephone she yelled at him until he hung up on her. We'd called her back when we returned because she'd told Hugh she'd get the police if we didn't. Even without the cops, the legal stuff began right away. Mom tried to get an order to prevent Dad from showing up. That got nowhere. Then Dad was advised to get some sort of order that would regularize his being able to see me, but that dragged on, and before it was resolved I was at Exeter and away from this mess.

I've talked so much about this short period to make it easier for you to understand what a huge, lifesaving relief it was to have that marriage end. Ever since I can remember, they had fought. Or rather, apropos of this or that she'd let him have it. Any subject would do. The way he drove was a big one. His tennis service—she thought he didn't throw the ball high enough and didn't have the right kind of follow-through, and she was right about that, but what could he do about it? He hadn't been taught right. The way he carved was lower class, especially leg of lamb and turkey. It had something to do with carving against the grain or with the grain, I can't remember which, and the way he held the knife. She'd tell him to observe Uncle John and Grandpa De Bourgh carefully; they were beautiful carvers. Wearing black shoes in daytime. That was a real no-no. It didn't matter how many times he told her it was the uniform on Wall Street. I'm only telling you about the out-in-the-open stuff. Other hollering had to do with what went on in the bedroom. Whatever that was, half the time Dad had to sleep in the guest bedroom. Sometimes she'd stand at the guest-room door and yell some more. Being in Little Compton with both of them was the worst. She rubbed it in all the time how it was her house, her furniture, her silverware, her club membership, her cousins, her friends. Even worse was the way she carried on when Dad took me to Newport to see his parents. Frankly, I don't know how he stood it. Grandpa Snow had sold the garage by then, so he mostly did crossword and jigsaw puzzles. Grandma was working as the bookkeeper or office manager for the new owner. They were nice people, very quiet and very dignified, living in a nice house that I liked. Mom of course had seen it, and you should hear her on the subject of the aluminum siding. They had tabby cats, sometimes two, sometimes three. Grandpa had had a couple of little strokes, so he dragged his left foot, but there was nothing wrong with his speech or his mind. Of course, they never showed up in Little Compton. They wouldn't have needed half their intelligence to figure out that Mom didn't want them on her property. Enough of this digression. I don't intend to knock Mom, but I think that by now you see that once that awful summer was over it was a relief not to live under the same roof with them.

By the beginning of the second term at school, they had worked out the separation agreement and when I could be with Dad, which was pretty much half of the regular weekends when I could get away from school and half of the summer vacations. Thanksgiving, Christmas, and Easter were always for Mom. She said she wanted me to spend them in proper circumstances, meaning with her, which was often a disaster because she'd not be feeling well or she'd made some plan that blew up, or in Bristol with Uncle John and Grandma and Grandpa De Bourgh if Mom hadn't just had one of her regular battle royals with them, after which usually months would pass without their speaking to one another.

Other parts I found strangely uplifting:

Then Dad hooked up with Jane, which was the best thing that ever happened to him and to me. That was during the winter before he and I came to see you and Aunt Bella on Île de Ré. I don't know whether you realized that he didn't bring her along, although she was already divorced, because he didn't want to give Mom a club with which to beat him and, I suppose, me over the head, meaning how he was exposing me to immoral behavior. They got married the following winter, but of course with the exception of that vacation I was seeing her each time I saw Dad. I didn't think I had ever known anyone so beautiful or so good, and after a while I realized that I was truly jealous of Dad. Whatever Freud or Jung has to say about it, I think more-or-less-stable boys, which by some miracle I was, really do accept the fact that their father sleeps with their mother. It's the way it is, a fundamental fact of life. With someone like Jane, who was so much younger than Dad and had no children, the knowledge that he was humping her, the word my friends and I seemed to favor, when they retired for the night or took an afternoon "nap," it was really heavy. I have no idea how it would have turned out, whether we could all three have had a good relationship, if Jane had not been so good to me, had not made me feel that I was as important to her as Dad. That sounds really stupid, but it's the truth. I assume it had to do with her not being able to have children of her own. God knows they tried. She hadn't managed to get pregnant when she was married to that jerk Horace, but she thought it might have been his fault, so with Dad they tried everything, all sorts of fertility treatments and even artificial insemination. It just didn't work. Dad offered to adopt, but she said, No, I don't need to, I have Jamie. So I've tried to be a son to her, and I wish I'd been able to give her more—for instance, by living on the East Coast, but that isn't where my work is, and I think she understands.

Then he came to what I thought was his real message, the real reason for writing the letter:

I never had any doubt that Dad loved me or was there to back me up. This became very important a couple of times when I screwed up at school, when I didn't get the sort of grades he'd gotten at Harvard where some of the professors still remembered him, and of course crucially important when I went out to Hollywood and began the routine of submitting work to agents without finding an agent who'd take me on or, once I had an agent, a director or producer who was interested. I'm not talking particularly about giving me money to live on without making a fuss over it. Why shouldn't he have? He'd become rich and didn't try to make a mystery of it. I'm talking about his liking my work and understanding it. Trying hard to understand it, which wasn't easy because he'd never watched television and his knowledge of popular culture was somewhere below zero. The crazy thing is that he got there and gave me comments and evaluations that were often way ahead of what I got from my agent or friends. I don't suppose I need to tell you that Jane was and is fabulous as a reader and adviser. She's a real pro, and she has the sort of sympathy or empathy that Dad had.

Then, when I met Stella and there was one of the bigger blowups with Mom, he kept his cool. Kept it with Mom, who was calling him five times a day telling him he had to stop me from ruining my life, and kept his cool with me. He avoided letting me fall into the trap of thinking that if Mom thinks I should stay away from Stella that is an imperative that says I've got to marry her ahora mismo. You may well ask what was so outrageously terrible about Stella, or perhaps you think you don't need to ask because I'm sure Mom has told you about the Chicana. But there is more to it than her being of Mexican descent or her parents having picked lettuce in Salinas or her being the first person in her family to go to the university. (By the way, she has a master's in mathematics and is a high school teacher.) Being the first person in your family to go to high school or college has become an American joke; I can't believe even Mom would run around telling her friends OMG, my daughter-in-law's parents only went through the tenth grade or whatever. No, the three major problems are that Stella isn't very white (peon color is what Mom calls it), that her parents have six other children, which meant I was letting myself in for marrying a whole tribe of peons, and finally that not only do the parents have no education but they also lack the redeeming get-up-and-go. Instead of owning a bodega or some functional equivalent by the time I met Stella, they owned a taco stand! By the way, they still own it, and they make mean tacos. Oh, and I forgot: the grandparents, the senior Garcias, were still alive! That problem has been three-quarters of the way solved. Stella's maternal grandfather is dead; both paternal grandparents are also dead; the grandmother lives with the parents. Now why do I tell you all this? It isn't to knock Mom. Given who she is, her obsession with the De Bourgh and Goddard family trees and Rhode Island history, you could hardly imagine her saying, Yippee, my only son is bringing diversity into the family. She'd already done that by marrying Dad! It's to offer a contrast. Dad, as you may or may not realize, for all his progressive, liberal, left-of-center, you name it, genuinely held views, was in his own much-quieter way a worse snob than Mom. For obvious reasons: he measured the distance he had traveled from the garage and didn't really like to see me "throwing it all away." He didn't tell me that, but I could read him. There was another problem so far as he was concerned—Mom had it too but to a much smaller extent, and I honestly don't know whether she had figured it out—and that was money. He and I didn't discuss money. He just gave it, usually without my asking. But when I told him I was quite serious about Stella, he said, among many very sweet things, that he was sure I understood that after he died I'd be rich, no, I think he actually said very well off, and I should be sure that the money I would inherit wouldn't distort my relations with Stella's family. "Distort" was the word. He said I should take care not to become the Garcia family piggy bank. So what I'm getting at is that at the end of the day Dad could see how deeply I loved Stella, and he studied her enough to see that she genuinely loved me, and once that was established he put his own pride and prejudices behind and decided to be really nice. By the way, he did manage it, as did Jane, who initially wasn't amused either. That was because they put me and my feelings first, and also because they could look into the future and see that if they had screwed it up with Stella they would have screwed it up with me.

On the other hand Mom could only consider her own feelings, principally her pride, and couldn't see the future. And here is another thing that is noteworthy. The way she acted was a contradiction of herself. Having known Mom for so many years you must know that she is the one who was the unconventional romantic, the occasional rebel and bad girl, while Dad when you come right down to it was always

the quintessential square who kept his nose clean and had no use for
eccentrics, bohemians, and weirdos and company.

I read Jamie's letter over twice, swam laps for exactly twenty minutes, and then drove to Salisbury for a cheeseburger and French fries followed by blueberry pie à la mode and coffee. This was more unhealthy food than I usually allowed myself in a week, but something inside me said, What the hell, eat what you want, have a second helping of fries, and, if you want a smoke, go for it, get a carton of Marlboros at the drugstore. The letterhead paper Jamie had used included a telephone number in the address. I called him when I got home, figuring that at twelve his time I had a good chance of catching him at the office. In fact it was his home number; a pleasant and friendly woman answered identifying herself as Stella. She said she knew exactly who I was, that Jamie would be very happy to speak with me, and that she would connect me to his cell phone. He was at his office, but she was sure that it was all right to disturb him. He picked up on the first ring, and as soon as she had heard him she hung up.

Jamie, I said, you've sent me an amazing letter. I hope your father realized how much you loved him and how well you understood him.

He made a noise that sounded like a grunt. I took it to be a substitute for yes, and he told me once more how very much he would have liked to see me. I replied that if he let me know when it would be convenient for me to visit him and Stella, whether before or after the baby was born, I'd be on my way. There was another grunt of assent, whereupon I asked how he was getting on with Lucy at present.

Ah well, he said, she has cooled her jets. Actually, she's said that she'd like to come out real soon after the baby is born. I think she has Christmas in mind. That's all right with us provided she understands that we will have Christmas dinner with the Garcia clan. Our house is big enough. The others don't have the space. I haven't sprung this concept on her yet, but I will before she gets herself all tangled up in plans. We'll see. The number one problem with her visits has been that we don't have her stay with us. Stella thinks we should, but I know Mom better. It would end badly. There are a couple of really good hotels right near us, and you'd think she'd really prefer to go to one of them; instead, she'd rather carry on about how she can't afford their prices. This time, if she really wants to come, I'll pay for the hotel and for a Hertz car and tell her it's her Christmas present. Period. Then if she decides she'd rather skip the Christmas meal with us and the Garcias she can eat there. Naturally I hope to hell it won't come to that.

Good luck! I said, and added that I had another question. Did he know the reason Thomas left Lucy—and him—at that particular time?

Jamie laughed. There are two versions, he told me, Mom's version and Dad's. Mom's version that she fed me for years is that she figured out he was cheating on her with Jane, and when she confronted him he flew into one of his rages, tried to kill her, and stormed out. I never believed that, because I happened to be there when Dad and Jane started dating, and that was more than a year after he left. I'd tell her that, but it was as though she didn't understand English. By the way, I've never witnessed one of those rages. They're also a part of Mom's foundation myth. Dad gave me his reason when I was already at college, having a difficult time, and working with a therapist. This woman made me focus on the way the feeling that I had been abandoned by Dad was tied up with some of my problems. So I asked him why he had left just then, and so brutally, without cushioning the blow for me, without making arrangements that would have spared me that awful summer. "Brutally" was the word I used. As you can imagine it was a painful conversation for both of us. He said he had learned that very day that she had been having an affair with someone who had been around before and that the sense of betrayal and humiliation was so strong that he felt compelled to act. I've never stopped regretting it, he added. Yes, I had to leave, no, there was no alternative, but I should have done it differently, I should have tried to do less harm. The funny thing is that later I figured out who this particular guy was. After Dad was gone he'd appear from time to time and telephone. He had a pretty unmistakable accent, and when I answered he'd just give his first name and ask for Mom. After they'd talked—she'd get me out of the room—she'd say, I have to go out. Then she'd disappear for the afternoon or evening if he called while I was in the city for some holiday, or if we were in Little Compton she'd say, I'm going into the city. Something has come up. I won't tell you his name, Jamie added. There's no point.

For a moment he fell silent.

Then he spoke again: Look, none of this matters anymore. It was the only time he hurt me, really hurt me, and how can I know that a slow exit, with all the fights and recriminations that would have surely taken place, was a better solution. And Mom? I don't blame her for having had an affair or any number of affairs. She was looking for something she couldn't find with Dad. His being a good guy, and having all those good qualities, was no substitute. She was very unhappy. The real point is that those two should have never been married. They should have never had a child.

You're nuts, I said. You have turned out magnificently well. Your father knew it. I hope that your mother's eyes will be opened. Perhaps they will if you carry through with your plan for Christmas.

I think of Bella constantly, not like the character in Proust's great novel who thinks of his dead wife often but only for brief moments at a time. Her presence is real, almost tangible. Regret that she is with her family at the cemetery in Montparnasse and not on my hillside in Sharon, where I hope Josiah will bury my ashes, comes over me in waves. I realize that it's childish and sentimental. Bella cannot know or care where I have laid her to rest, the place, be it said, that she had chosen. Neither she nor I will know or care about the eternal solitude of my bones. So in reality it must be that I mourn the extinction upon my death of the memory of the happiness we had shared. Our happiness which, now that she is dead, has become inalterable, a loss that no hope, such as the one that may have comforted Proust, that our books will be for some time still displayed in bookstore windows and on library shelves, can compensate. The fights and recriminations of which Jamie had spoken? They were as alien to me as the customs of the most isolated Amazon tribes Lévi-Strauss had cataloged in *Tristes Tropiques*. Bella and I had never fought. At times I found myself tormented by the realization that I had behaved foolishly or that she had misunderstood my actions and motives or that she or I might have been less rigid in the response to this or that contingency, but we learned to regain our serenity quickly, and no residue of bitterness was left, in any event not in me. The gods seized and destroyed our little Agnes. Was that the price we paid for their blessing?

I was reading in the *NYT* about the bomb that had exploded outside the Shia shrine in Najaf, the most important one to Iraqi Shiites. The dead numbered about one hundred, among them an ayatollah long opposed to Saddam and helpful in building support for Americans. The damage to the building itself was said to be considerable. The telephone rang, startling me: practically everyone I knew had abandoned the telephone in favor of e-mail. The caller was Lucy. She was in Little Compton, bored and as annoyed as hell. Her Goddard cousins hadn't invited her to their Labor Day picnic. She'd been stewing about it, wondering whether she shouldn't scoot over to New York so as not to lose face, and then she thought of me. It was the last minute, but could I have her for the Labor Day weekend? She'd be there the next day. Don't worry, she added, I'll leave on Tuesday. We'll have a good time, like in the old days.

She sounded like the old Lucy: gay, chatty, and faintly rambunctious. I told her that of course I'd be delighted to have her, but she should realize that I had no social life to speak of, and while my TV set had worked when last turned on I could provide no other entertainments.

I'll be there in time for drinks, she replied, and asked for directions.

It was a welcome surprise to observe after she arrived how different she seemed from the woman whose wrenching reminiscences and commentary I had been listening to in the course of all those conversations in May and June. The hectoring, accusatory tone was gone; she cracked jokes about the summer's goings-on at the club in Little Compton; the harrowing Fourth of July visit to her brother John's at the Ausable Club; being cut dead by Priscilla van Buren at the little Vanderbilt's engagement party in Newport. Her appearance was improved as well. Was it the combination of the suntan and a new pink lipstick? I couldn't tell, but she looked younger and less hard, validating the memory I had preserved of her from the fifties in Paris. I took a leaf out of her book that evening and for dinner gave her cold fried chicken I'd bought at the market in the afternoon, tomato salad, cheese that I happened to have in the fridge, and melon. She ate cheerfully, drank almost a whole bottle of wine, declined my offer of coffee, and traipsed off to bed. I had warned her that during the day I would be working, that lunch would consist of sardines or canned tuna, and that until it was time for drinks she would be on her own. That's just fine, she had told me.

I've never been able to concentrate exclusively on a text. During the many minutes I wasted goofing off I couldn't help being pleasantly aware that she spent a good couple of hours at the swimming pool—doing laps, she told me later, and afterward soaking up the sun—and, after she had knocked on my door and asked whether I would mind if she weeded and deadheaded the flower beds, that she gave over most of the afternoon to doing just that. Bella's task, I thought. How jarring that this woman should have undertaken it. Jarring and normal: it was, I realized, what any woman accustomed to having a garden and working in it would do if she were left to her own devices and saw the orphaned condition of the flower beds.

Uncertain about just how rocky the visit might turn out to be, and believing strongly in the moderating influence that strangers Lucy might like to impress would have on her, I had called, as soon as she announced her arrival, my former tenant, Bard professor Peter Drummond, and invited him and his partner to dinner. They were free. Miraculously, Mrs. James was as well, and to make her life and mine as easy as possible, I asked her to bring an entire cold dinner that she would prepare at home. Experience had taught me that she much preferred that to cooking in my kitchen and having me interfere. She proposed roast pork, pasta salad, a green salad, and one of her daughter's fruit tarts. That is what we had.

Lucy's social skills, which she had displayed to such good

effect when she gave her little dinners in Paris, had not deserted her. She drew out Peter about his work. He told us he had written his doctoral dissertation on nineteenth-century American nativist tradition and was doing research on today's Fundamentalist Christians and their morphing into a far-right movement.

That discussion, accompanied by the obligatory jeremiads about George W. and his mismanaged wars, carried us through the peach tart. As we were having coffee in the living room, Lucy turned her attention to Peter's partner, Ezra. She opened my piano, played a scale, made a face, and asked Ezra whether he could bear to play one of his pieces on an instrument that was so out of tune. It's all dissonance anyway, he replied. I'll give it a whirl.

I didn't expect to see her at breakfast the next morning. It was late when we said good night, and once more too much wine had been drunk, followed in Lucy's case by a nightcap or perhaps even two. In fact, she stuck her head into my study not long before lunch and said she would work off the excesses of the previous evening in the pool. I told her to swim or sun herself as long as she liked and to let me know when she had finished. We had lunch correspondingly late. I had done more than enough work during the long morning session, and when she asked whether I would mind having coffee after lunch out in the garden I gladly agreed. We sat down in the wooden armchairs on the back lawn, where the shade was already deep. She was smoking. When she offered me a cigarette I accepted, mindful of the advice I had given myself to loosen up.

You've got a nice house, she told me, and a pleasant life. I like the way you organize things. This is a new, very domesticated Philip.

I replied that in reality I was simply following precedent, doing things in Sharon as much as possible the way Bella had done them.

Evidently, she was a good teacher. I wish I had known her better.

I nodded. There was no use reminding her that at the time they had been like oil and water.

I was startled when she next asked me whether my books sold well. I mean, she added, that I don't see them on bestseller lists. Of course I know about the prizes and the honors.

It depends on your point of view, I told her. My early books sold better. I had an audience that was larger, I appealed more to young people. The sales figures are still respectable in the U.S. Sometimes they're better abroad. Let's say that I'm not dissatisfied or embarrassed, but on the other hand my publishers wouldn't think the roof had fallen in if it became obvious that I would never submit another novel. They don't make enough money on me to care.

That's pretty much what I imagined, said Lucy, although I have really enjoyed some of your books. I've even read a couple more than once. You know, *The Happy Monsters*. That was really close to the bone. Close to the De Bourgh family!

She was referring to my coming-of-age novel, in which I had worked over my own family, placing it in Salem, where my ancestors have lived since before the witch trials.

As I've looked around here, she continued, I got the

impression—I hope you won't mind my saying so—that it would be good to spend some more money on the house. You know, the kitchen could be modernized; you could have quieter and more efficient machines. The same goes for your pool filter and heater. If I were you, I'd replace them. The propane heater I've had installed in Little Compton is absolutely silent. It's such a relief! But I suppose you're being careful.

There is some of that, I said. There is also the question of my age. How much longer will I be around? Is there any point in making myself a present of one of those German dishwashers that can also do windows and detail my car?

Philip, she said, may I move closer to you?

I got up and instead moved my chair.

The truth is, she continued, that even though I complain about how first Father, then John, butchered our family accounts, I'm still quite rich. Richer than you think. And I'm not really a bitch. I've told you so much about myself that you must think I am, but that's not the truth. I'm in good shape now—in my head and in the rest of the body. I could give you a nice life—sex included. So what do you say, old friend?

I looked at her. As she had said, she was in good shape, and one could imagine having a good time with her. It was too bad. I smiled at her as nicely as I knew how and shook my head.

Memories of a Marriage

LOUIS BEGLEY

A Reader's Guide

Love Is All You Need

by Louis Begley

Memories of a Marriage was born out of years of brooding over the marriages of the few college classmates I have kept up with and of other friends and acquaintances more or less my age.

Many, perhaps most, of these marriages have failed, some early on and some not so long ago. If a reason could be identified, it has usually been a spouse's unwillingness to tolerate the infidelity of the other, or (alternatively) a spouse's insistence on leaving for someone else—for someone of the same sex, in several cases of late-blooming self-discovery. There has been nothing as threatening among my friends as physical abuse by a spouse, or one of the spouses' alcoholism, drug addiction, or compulsive gambling, or falling afoul of criminal laws. I have, however, observed marriages such as that of Lucy De Bourgh and Thomas Snow, the central figures of *Memories of a Marriage*: marriages that have disintegrated, ostensibly without a compelling reason, amid the debris of silent hostility or recriminations. Marriages of nice prosperous people, no sword of Damocles hanging over their heads, but somehow or other you know that their marriage is not happy. One day they invite you to dinner or Sunday lunch at their apartment, or perhaps to spend the weekend at their place in the country, but, when you see them some weeks or months later, they abjure any thought of living with that Monster! And pretty soon one or the other of them makes it amply clear that the war between them isn't only over money, or the custody of the children (if, as it too often happens, there are children in the picture young enough to be fought over), or that comfortable apartment or house in the country, or the art they've collected together, but also over friends. You're with me or against me. Forget about seeing me if you go on seeing him—or her—becomes the battle cry. Don't you realize that the Monster has wrecked my life?

We are all, of course, amateur psychotherapists, and, aided by hindsight, we zero in on the hidden reason. It was inevitable, we say. She's unstable, he's a compulsive control freak, all she knows how to do is shop, all he's good for are all-nighters at the office, he's depressive, she's bipolar. . . . In the old days, before the advent of no-fault, it all came down to incompatibility and mental cruelty, those were the workhorse grounds alleged by rote in quickie Reno divorces. Those diagnoses may not be wrong, but what went on between Joe and Jane or Dick and Dawn during the years when they seemed just fine and had the children? There are answers to that question, which likewise may not be wrong: They got married because they were lonely, or because of the great sex, or because they wanted children, or because Dick had hoped to use Dawn (or was it Dawn who intended to use Dick?) as a stepping-stone to a better life. It was all a big mistake, but they had been hanging in, trying to make a go of it. Finally something inside one or both of them snapped. Not infrequently, suddenly having more money than in the past has made it easier to decide it was time to call it quits.

"Let me not to the marriage of true minds / Admit impediments . . . ," Shakespeare wrote in Sonnet 116. In that context, steadfast in allegiance, faithful, and loyal are probably the most relevant definitions of "true." Were Lucy's and Thomas's minds "true"? Shakespeare went on to throw down his gauntlet: "If this be error and upon me proved, / I never writ, nor no man ever loved." Does what he said hold if among the "impediments" is real or fancied inequality between the lovers? Do lovers who are "true" overlook or rise above it? Is it possible that in this instance the Bard was wrong? Or were Lucy's and Thomas's minds not "true": hers because she was incurably snobbish and ungenerous, and his because the catnip that drew him was not only sex with her, but also her wealth and social position? Inequality in marriages has ever been grist for novelists' and playwrights' mills. It shouldn't come as a surprise that these questions have been swirling in my head.

For all the traditional reasons—her family's importance in the history of Rhode Island and of the nation, and its wealth and distinction—Lucy believes she is at the summit of American society. If she had thought of it, she might have said she was an American orchid. For equally traditional reasons,

Thomas, the son of a garage owner and his bookkeeper wife, belongs to the lower class. To add insult to injury, the garage is in Newport, the most elegant of summer resorts, only a hop, skip, and a jump from the De Bourgh ancestral mansion in Bristol, R.I. This makes Thomas, who might have gassed up the fancy cars of Lucy's friends, a "townie," a disqualifying and faintly ludicrous condition that his Harvard College, London School of Economics, and Harvard Business School degrees and his good looks and good manners can at best mask from eyes less discerning than hers. A point not to be missed in this equation is that, until he finally leaves her, Thomas tacitly accepts Lucy's assessment of their relative status. I added, for good measure, other irritants such Lucy's low opinion of Thomas's sexual prowess and his being a square with hardly any interest in the arts. But I have the impression that Lucy would have been more tolerant of such failings in a man of her own caste.

What would have been required, I asked myself, for Lucy to come off it, to stop snubbing her own husband, to forgive the garage and the aluminum siding on Thomas's parental home? I am aware that the class system in which Lucy and Thomas grew up is no longer the American norm, but my inquiry is not moot. Couples continue to face the impediment of inequality in other forms, some old as the world and some new. Among the old: disparity of fortune, education, and looks (a conspicuously handsome spouse married to an ugly duckling). An inequality that Lucy perceived: One partner is a sex athlete, and the other is an underperformer. A new form of inequality that afflicts more and more couples is that of uneven advancement in the spouses' respective careers. It used to be that husbands had careers and wives took care of the children and made sure the household ran to the husband's satisfaction. Or, if the wife had a job, her job was understood to be the source of a second income rather than to represent a career that counted. That time is past; two-career families are rapidly becoming the norm, and the woman who succeeds better than her husband, rising higher in business or a profession, is no longer a rare bird. Stay-at-home dads are a recognized species. Why do some couples shrug off—or adjust to—these disparities while others, like Lucy and Thomas, founder?

Steadfastness and loyalty (and I would add generosity): I'm not sure that Lucy, of whom I'm very fond because I have a soft spot in my heart for wild girls, possesses those qualities in great abundance. And then there is the formulation offered by Alex van Buren in the course of his long interview with Philip, which is that, fundamentally, Lucy didn't like Thomas. Without simple affection, says Alex, not sex but simple affection, a marriage can't work.

For my part, I believe that Alex is far from wrong.

Questions and Topics for Discussion

1. *Memories of a Marriage* opens in May 2003, "not many days after George W. Bush's astonishing announcement that the 'mission' had been accomplished." Why do you think the novel is set when it is? How does this historical moment—with its questions of whether politicians tell us the truth, and when to believe them—resonate with the story that Philip is about to tell?

2. We learn early in the book that Philip and Bella lost their only child, Agnes, in a tragic accident—and thereafter avoided New York City, where she died. How do you think such a loss would affect a marriage? Do you understand their decision to leave?

3. Lucy comes from privilege and a well-connected family; Thomas's family operates a garage. But by the time the novel begins their positions have reversed. Thomas died rich and

vastly successful as an investment banker. Lucy's fortune hasn't kept pace, and she thinks of herself as "an unglamorous boring old woman" whom no one wants at their table. Do you think their changing fortunes represent a bigger shift in American society? How do we measure success and status today, as opposed to when Lucy and Thomas first met?

4. When Philip visits Lucy at her apartment, she tells him that she's lonely, and that her life is not "what I had once expected." What do you think she imagined for herself? Does her disappointment make her a more sympathetic character?

5. As Lucy tells Philip about her marriage to Thomas, she also describes her long-standing, passionate affair with Hubert. This is not the only adulterous love mentioned in the novel; when Philip falls for Bella, she is married to another man. Is adultery ever acceptable? What do you think of these relationships?

6. Philip is an author. When he first meets Bella, he tells her that his novels explore "love and ambition, and betrayal and fear of the ravages of old age." Do you think this is a good description of *Memories of a Marriage*? If you've read other books by Louis Begley, do you see an overlap between Philip's work and Begley's own?

7. Near the end of the novel we learn the title of one other novel Philip has written: *The Happy Monsters*, a roman à clef set

in Salem, Massachusetts. Why do you think Begley reveals the title and subject of this particular novel? What is a "happy monster," and do any of the characters in *Memories of a Marriage* fit that description?

8. To whose marriage do you think the title refers? Lucy and Thomas's—obviously the subject of Philip's investigation—or Philip and Bella's, which he mentions throughout?

9. Lucy and Philip had a brief fling in France, before she met Thomas. At the end of the novel, she suggests reigniting their affair. Why do you think Philip turns her down?

10. Philip discusses Lucy and Thomas's marriage with many people: Lucy herself; Jane, Thomas's widow; Jamie, Lucy and Thomas's son; Josiah, Thomas's acquaintance and Philip's cousin; and Alex Van Buren and Bill Taylor, mutual friends. Do you trust any of these confidants? Why or why not?

11. When Philip renews his acquaintance with Lucy he is shocked to hear her refer to Thomas as "that monster." By the end of the novel, do you think Philip believes her? Do you believe her? Why do you think her marriage with Thomas fell apart?

12. What makes a good marriage? Are any of the couples in the novel—Lucy and Thomas, Jane and Ned, Philip and Bella, among others—models for a strong marriage?

13. What do you think happens after the novel ends? Has Philip learned everything he wants to? Does he write his book about Lucy and Thomas's marriage? Are we to think *Memories of a Marriage* is that book?

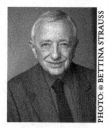

Louis Begley's previous novels are *Schmidt Steps Back, Matters of Honor, Shipwreck, Schmidt Delivered, Mistler's Exit, About Schmidt, As Max Saw It, The Man Who Was Late,* and *Wartime Lies,* which won the Hemingway/PEN award and the Irish Times-Aer Lingus International Fiction Prize and was a finalist for the National Book Award. His work has been translated into eighteen languages.

Printed in the United States
by Baker & Taylor Publisher Services

Printed in the United States
by Baker & Taylor Publisher Services